No. It couldn't be. It couldn't...

Jax blinked and scrubbed a hand down his face.

There was no mistaking the sound of distinctive, distraught mewling coming from two tiny swaddled infants, bundled into their car seats and blocking the front door of his cabin.

Babies?

He crouched before the baby on his left, gently adjusting the pink blanket covering her and making what he hoped were calming shushing noises. His expertise was horses. He knew zero about babies.

She was incredibly tiny next to his large palm. So vulnerable. So defenseless. He swallowed hard.

Susie had left two helpless infants on his front porch? She'd always been irresponsible and often acted with poor judgment, but this went far beyond the pale even for her.

"Jax?" Faith asked. She knelt before the other baby and gently rocked the seat to calm the infant. "Are these…?"

"I don't— I'm not—" Jax stammered, his head spinning. His emotions rarely got the better of him. But right now he was fighting with every ounce of his courage against succumbing to the conflicting feelings pelting him.

Shock. Surprise. Anger. Betrayal. Guilt. Pain.

Wonder.

Award-winning author **Deb Kastner** lives and writes in beautiful Colorado. Since her daughters have grown into adulthood and her nest is almost empty, she is excited to be able to discover new adventures, challenges and blessings, the biggest of which is her sweet grandchildren. She enjoys reading, watching movies, listening to music, singing in the church choir, and attending concerts and musicals.

Visit the Author Profile page at Harlequin.com for more titles.

The Cowboy's Twins

Deb Kastner

Recycling programs
for this product may
not exist in your area.

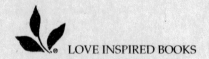

LOVE INSPIRED BOOKS

ISBN-13: 978-0-373-81907-2

The Cowboy's Twins

Copyright © 2016 by Debra Kastner

www.Harlequin.com

Printed in U.S.A.

Now may our Lord Jesus Christ Himself, and our God and Father, who has loved us and given us everlasting consolation and good hope by grace, comfort your hearts and establish you in every good word and work.

—*2 Thessalonians* 2:16–17

To my husband, Joe, who demonstrates every day what it means to be a loving, God-fearing man. You are an excellent male role model and I join with your children and grandchildren in proclaiming you the best Daddy and Grampy ever. I couldn't write these stories about men of faith without you to inspire me.

And to my sister at Happy Haven Farm and Sanctuary, for the work you do rescuing horses (and dogs, and cats, and goats, and everything else with fur). Thank you for all your help with my research into the plight of wild horses. Any mistakes are entirely my own.

Chapter One

There was only one conceivable reason why Jax McKenna would ever consider putting himself at Serendipity, Texas's Bachelors and Baskets auction like a mule among thoroughbreds—and it *wasn't* because his loudmouthed brothers, Slade and Nick, were forcing him into it.

Nor was it the sweet talking of Jo Spencer, the spry, seventy-something redhead who owned the town's only public eatery, Cup O' Jo's Café. She was the one who'd organized the event in the first place and she was pretty much capable of talking anyone into anything—but it hadn't been necessary this time. Not with Jax.

They all might think they were strong-arming him, but if he hadn't ultimately made the final decision to do this, he wouldn't be here, and no amount of coercing or cajoling on their part would have seen him do otherwise.

He'd made the choice to be here because the fundraiser was important to him. He'd do his bit to help it succeed, even if it meant humiliating himself in front of the town. But that didn't mean he had to be happy about it.

He scoffed quietly and glared at Slade, whose lips twitched to keep back a grin. Jax's scowl deepened.

"Settle down, people. Settle down." Jo spoke directly into the microphone, cringed at the earsplitting feedback and flipped it off. It wasn't as if she needed the thing. Her voice easily carried across the distance of Serendipity, Texas's community green, where practically everyone in town had gathered for this *event*. "Time to get this party started."

Jax crossed his arms over his chest and grunted. Since when was pure torture considered a festive occasion?

Today, apparently.

When the ruckus didn't immediately subside, old Frank Spencer—Jo's crotchety husband—put his fingers to his lips and whistled shrilly. "Listen up, folks. The First Annual Bachelors and Baskets Auction is about to begin. Gather 'round, y'all."

Jax crushed the toe of his tan cowboy boot

into the soft grass, wishing he was anywhere else. Where did Jo come up with this silly idea, anyway? It wasn't like any auction he had ever heard of, although he didn't know why he was so surprised by the fact. Serendipity wasn't exactly known for being *normal* with anything, especially with Jo Spencer at the helm.

What had started out as Jo's simple if archaic idea to pawn off the single men for money had grown into something much larger and more complex. She might have originally set out to nab the town bachelors, but her idea had spun so far out of control that now nearly every man in town was lined up to strut his stuff, single and married alike. Now, the idea was that the women could bid on men for *tasks* instead of dates—with the tasks to be determined by the winning bidder.

Want someone to do the cooking for your barbecue party next weekend? Bid on the man with the secret-family-recipe barbecue sauce that he refused to share with a soul. Want someone to fix up that rusting old truck in your barn? Bid on the town mechanic, and he'll get it running like new. Or go ahead and bid on your husband or sweetheart…and then put him to work. Jax had overheard one woman saying that when she won her husband, she was going to make him clean out the garage, the way he'd been promising to do for the past five years.

The new twist meant that anyone could participate, even if he was already married or dating. Apparently, Jo figured the more men, the more money would be raised, and Jax supposed there was some truth to that. He just wished he wasn't wrapped up in it. With this many men, did they really need him?

He scoffed under his breath. Tell folks they were meeting for a good cause and they showed up in spades. Actually, just tell people there was a party. *Any* reason to celebrate was reason enough for Serendipity, and the fact that the auction was to benefit the building fund for the new town council–approved senior center and hospice was icing on the cake. It *was* a good cause—one close to his heart, which was the only reason Jax had come out this morning.

Not to be outdone, the ladies in town had started offering to bring picnic baskets to share with the men they won in the auction. Then the event had morphed into bachelors and baskets—which was catchy, even if it was far from accurate, since a good half of the men being auctioned off were married or in serious relationships. If nothing else, Jax was looking forward to the food. He never turned down a good meal. Delicious, down-home country cooking. Too bad he had to put himself through such a ridiculous spectacle just to be able to fill his belly.

Slade nudged Jax with his elbow. "Who do you think is gonna bid on you?"

"How should I know?" Jax snapped derisively. He didn't expect much. He didn't expect anything at all. Most likely he was going to stand up on the stage and make a fool of himself for nothing. No woman in her right mind would bid on his ugly mug, no matter how worthy the cause.

"I can't wait to eat Laney's picnic lunch. She packed fried chicken." Slade licked his lips in an overstated motion that made Jax want to snort in exasperation. For a moment he wished he were Slade, who knew exactly whom he'd be spending the day with—his wife. Slade and Laney were expecting a child in the fall, a baby sister for two-year-old Brody, but they still acted like a couple of goofy newlyweds.

"You sure she's gonna bid on you, baby brother?" Nick goaded, bumping Slade's shoulder with his. "Maybe she'll take your money and bid on a handsome man—like me, for example." He chuckled.

Nick was a big bear of a man with a grouchy personality to match, but he knew how to turn on the charm when he wanted to and he was no slouch with the ladies. Laney might favor her own husband over Nick, but there was no doubt Nick would get his fair share of interest at the auction. He'd get bid on, or bought or whatever crazy word they were using for it.

Slade winked and flashed his wedding ring at his brothers. "I have it on good authority that it's a done deal."

Jax wanted to slug the self-satisfied look right off Slade's face. Just because he was happy with his married life didn't mean the rest of the world had to suffer his gloating. Especially when Slade knew that the topic of marriage was still a tender wound for Jax right now.

Jo pounded a gavel—probably the same one her town-council president husband, Frank, used—on the podium in front of her.

"First up, I'd like to offer Slade McKenna to our viewing public."

Slade flashed his brothers a confident grin and stepped onto the platform. He tipped his hat to the roaring crowd and then flexed his biceps for good measure.

Seriously? If anyone—*anyone*—thought

Jax was going to get up on that stage and make a raging fool out of himself like his brother was doing…yeah, that was so not happening.

The crowd roared with delight, hooting and hollering. Actually encouraging Slade, as if he needed a bigger ego than he already had.

"Look at the strength in those shoulders," Jo said, punctuating her statement with a hoot of her own. "Former bull rider and current member of our esteemed police force, Slade will pitch in and use that brawn and brute strength for any project of your choosing. Laney, dear, would you like to open up the bidding?" Jo suggested with a chuckle. "Surely you must want this handsome hunk all to yourself."

Jax thought it was silly for Laney to bid on her own husband. Slade was pretty much at her beck and call anyway, and all she had to do was smile at him—it didn't cost her a dime.

"Oh, I have the perfect project for him." Laney jumped in without a moment's hesitation. "Dishes and laundry for a month."

Slade groaned. "Really?"

Jax chuckled. Served his brother right for being so cocky.

"Three hundred dollars," Laney offered, already halfway up to the podium. There was no question that she was the clear winner of *this* particular item.

Alexis Haddon, a local rancher and part of the fundraising committee, stood at the foot of the stairs, waiting to pass a lariat to Laney.

"Make it a good one, darlin'," Slade coaxed his wife with a sideways grin.

She whooped and swung the lariat toward Slade. Jax scoffed under his breath. Laney wouldn't be able to rope the broad side of a barn with technique like that—or rather, total lack of technique.

She gave her best effort but the lariat soared a good couple of feet past Slade's head. She yanked on the end of the rope in a vain attempt to correct her overthrow but to no avail. She would have come up empty-handed were it not for Slade's quick thinking. He dived for the loop and slipped it over his head, then rolled toward her until he was completely wound up in the line.

"Guess you caught me," Slade said, laughing with the crowd.

Jax shook his head. He had to give his little brother props for putting on a good show. Even when he was little he had loved to be in the limelight, the center of attention. Probably because he was the baby of the family.

Over the din, Frank stepped up to the podium and grabbed the gavel from Jo's hand, pounding it against the podium. "Now, see here. Jo never even got to say he was sold yet, and y'all are already draggin' him off the stage? Let's have some order to these here proceedings."

Jo snorted and grabbed the gavel back from him. "Go sit down, old man," she demanded, giving his grizzled cheek an affectionate buss. "Everyone knew from the get-go that Slade's wife was going to win him. Now you just be good and wait your turn, or *your* wife might just leave you a-hanging."

Honestly, Jax didn't know how Frank and Jo managed to live together without killing one another, but at the heart of it, their unconventional love for each other worked for them.

If Jax had had half the wisdom and foresight that this old couple shared, maybe his own marriage would have—

"Jax McKenna."

The sound of his name pierced into his thoughts like a dart popping a balloon.

Nick gave him a none-too-gentle shove. "You're up, bro. Go get 'em."

"No, I—" Jax protested. He wasn't ready to be paraded around like a piece of prime horseflesh. Not that he would ever be ready to face this moment, but he'd at least hoped to have a little more time to get used to the idea, to see how it went with some of the other guys before it was his turn to go.

With reluctant steps he dragged himself onto the platform, his jaw, his fists and his stomach clenched so tight he thought he might be sick. Folks were staring at him, and though the rational part of him knew that he was imagining it, he felt as if everyone's gaze was glued to the ragged scar that ran from the corner of his mouth to his left temple.

He'd never been overly concerned about his appearance—at least not until after his face had been scarred in an accident and his wife, Susie, had left him for another man. The pain of his divorce was still too fresh for him to ignore, on top of the pain of the scars that marked him both inside and out, marring his features, badly damaging his hearing and shattering his confidence in himself. Everything combined to make participating in this auction all the more excruciating, no matter how good the cause.

He turned and started back the way he came. They had plenty of guys willing and able to compete in the auction. They would do just fine without him. He wouldn't fetch much of a price, anyway.

"Jackson Daniel McKenna, you freeze right where you are." Jax might be deaf in one ear, but that was no obstacle to Jo Spencer. Jax firmly believed her voice was loud enough and powerful enough to pierce through a stone wall, if she set her mind to it. And in this instance, it stopped him dead in his tracks. She was like a second mother to most of the town, Jax included, and her tone brooked no nonsense, making him feel as if he was a troublemaking five-year-old all over again.

"Turn your cute little fanny around and get on back over here, son. We need all the genuine bachelors we can get in this here auction. There might be a lady out there who's just been waiting for an opportunity like this to get to know you, handsome fellow that you are."

Jax flinched inwardly. He was one *bachelor* Serendipity could do without.

But denying Jo what she wanted? He couldn't do that, especially in front of a crowd. He was painfully aware he was making an even bigger spectacle of himself by balking on the stage.

"Yes, ma'am," he muttered, heading toward the front of the stage, dragging his feet with every step. When he got there, he stood stock-still, as if he was facing a firing squad. It kind of felt that way. There was no laughter or cheers this time, as there had been with his brother. That was fine by Jax. He might have to give in to Jo's prodding, but he would not—*not*—flex his muscles the way Slade had done. He pulled the brim of his tan cowboy hat down lower over his eyes and jammed his hands in the front pockets of his blue jeans for good measure.

"Who is going to start the bidding for us today on this fine specimen of a man?" She gestured for him to pose like Slade had done but Jax ignored her. "Just look at the size of him. Which lovely young lady out there has some heavy lifting they need Jax here to do for them?"

The assembly was deathly silent—exactly as Jax had expected. No surprise there. He could hear his own breath, loud and ragged, scratching through the hush of the crowd.

He wanted to curl in on himself, but instead he straightened his shoulders. He wouldn't cower, nor would he let anyone know how difficult this was for him. If he stood still long enough, the charade would play itself out and be over in a minute.

No one would bid on him. He'd swallow his pride and humiliation and go back to his ranch where he belonged. At least there he could find a semblance of peace among his award-winning herd of quarter horses, bred and trained for the rodeo circuit.

"Don't tell me there's not a-one of you ladies out there who needs a few chores done around your houses or ranches—something that requires a big, strapping man? Moving boxes, maybe? Bales of hay?"

Still nothing. Just the rustling sound of a few awkwardly shifting feet. A cough or two.

Jax caught Jo's gaze, silently begging her to shoot him now and put him out of his misery. Honestly, he'd be willing to cough up a couple of hundred bucks out of his own pocket if it meant he could just walk away.

Jo frowned, lifted her chin and shook her head.

Stubborn old woman.

"I know most of y'all already know this about him, but he's a wonder with horses. Top-notch. Anyone have a horse that needs training?"

This was ridiculous. Jax had had enough, and no doubt the crowd had, too. They were a nice enough bunch and they were probably feeling a whole lot of sorry for him right now.

Well, he didn't want their pity.

"Five," came a sweet, soft soprano located

somewhere near the back of the crowd. Jax didn't believe he recognized the woman's voice, which was odd, since he knew most everyone in the small town.

"I'm sorry, dear," Jo said, cupping a hand to her ear. "You'll have to speak up. I couldn't quite make out what you said."

"Five," the voice repeated, stronger and nearer to the platform now. "Hundred. Dollars. Five hundred dollars for the cowboy."

Half a grand? For him?

Jax scanned the crowd until his gaze locked on the clearest, most sparkling hazel eyes he'd ever seen. The gaze belonged to a tall, lithe, blond-haired young lady who'd finally managed to work her way to the front of the crowd.

He'd definitely never seen her before. No way would he forget the kind of beauty she possessed. She looked as if she'd just walked off the cover of one of those fancy New York fashion magazines. Dressed that way, too, with a poofy purple scarf wound multiple times around her supple neck, a silky emerald shirt and designer jeans that emphasized her long legs but had definitely never seen the back of a horse. Most telling were her three-inch spiked heels that sunk into the soft grass with every step.

The woman actually had cash in her hand—five crisp Benjamin Franklins, which she waved in the air like a flag.

"Five hundred dollars," she repeated for the third time. "But please, don't make me lasso the poor man."

The woman operating the cash box flashed Faith Dugan a welcome smile as Faith pressed five hundred-dollar bills into her palm. She hadn't had time to visit the local branch of Serendipity's bank to establish a checking account, and she felt awkward waving around that kind of cash. Apparently, she looked awkward, too—which she imagined was the reason all eyes were now upon her.

That and the fact that she was a newcomer in a crowd of people who had no doubt been born and raised in this town. Serendipity, Texas, wasn't the kind of place folks moved in and out of. She was the exception. And she seemed to have shocked everyone by shelling out five hundred dollars for the brooding cowboy.

Faith wasn't trying to impress anyone. She just needed help rebuilding her newly purchased ranch property, which she hoped soon would be a bona fide mustang rescue.

"You're new in town?" the woman asked.

"Jo mentioned we had a new resident. I'm glad to meet you. I'm Alexis Haddon. You're going to love living in Serendipity." To Faith's surprise, Alexis pulled her into an exuberant hug, as if they were old friends. She'd had plenty of smiles and welcomes in the few days she'd been in town. Folks around here sure were outgoing and friendly. It was nothing like large, busy and somewhat impersonal Hartford, Connecticut, where she'd been born and raised.

"Thank you." Faith hoped her response to Alexis's hug didn't appear as awkward as she felt. "I'm Faith Dugan. I just bought the Dennys' old property."

Excitement bubbled up inside her every time she thought about her plans for the place, but she bit her tongue to keep from bursting out her intentions. Now was hardly the time to get into her reasons for settling in town.

Alexis blew out a low whistle. "I'd heard that someone had picked up the place. You sure chose a fixer-upper. I hope you enjoy a challenge. Old man Denny was an eighty-five-year-old widower, and his health got so poor that he couldn't work the place himself for the last ten years of his life. He didn't have any family, and he was in a senior center in

San Antonio for the last couple of years. His ranch just sat there vacant. Such a shame."

Despite her eagerness for the project, Faith cringed inwardly at the reminder of the size of the task ahead of her. She'd been evaluating the ranch for repairs, but she'd hoped it wasn't in quite as bad of shape as it seemed. Apparently, her assessment had been fairly accurate. There was a reason the asking price for the property had been well under market value. It was going to take a lot of work to get her new ranch into running condition so she could host the herd of wild mustangs she intended to save.

But that was fine—she was up for the challenge. She wasn't going to let a little hard work put her off her dreams.

"People like Mr. Denny are the reason we're holding the auction today," Alexis went on. "So we can build a senior center and hospice here in town. Poor Mr. Denny wouldn't have had to have spent his last years so far away from the town he was born and raised in if we'd had a facility available. It wouldn't have made any difference to the state of his ranch, of course, but he could have come to church, spent time with some familiar faces. Serendipity folk like to take care of their own."

"It's a good cause," Faith agreed, offering

up a silent prayer for Mr. Denny, the poor man who'd died alone, far from his home. She knew what it felt like to be lonely.

"We appreciate your generosity, bidding in our auction," Alexis continued with her vibrant, upbeat chatter, "especially since you're a newcomer. I'm sure your neighbors will be around to introduce themselves to you if they haven't already. Everyone is a friend here. As an added bonus, you've won Jax. You've made a good choice. He's a big ol' brute, but don't let that scare you off. He has a heart of gold and those muscles of his were earned through hard labor. He knows ranching backward and forward. I'm sure you'll find plenty of uses for him at the ranch."

Faith wasn't certain how Jax would feel about Alexis's summation of his capabilities and value. Faith had a hard time picturing Jax with a heart of *gold* given the sheen of ice obscuring his dark brown eyes.

She didn't require his heart for this job, nor did she have any interest in what color it was. What she needed was a pair of strong arms and maybe some good advice from someone who knew his way around a ranch. Jo had mentioned Jax was good with horses. If he could also pound nails and mend fences, so much the better.

She would have had to hire someone to do the work, anyway. How awesome was it that her money would be doing double duty? She'd get the help she needed—for a little while, anyway—and the town would get its senior center built.

Win, win.

Though poor Jax sure didn't seem to think he'd won anything.

He definitely hadn't looked as if he'd wanted to be standing on a platform hawking himself, but she was sure he hadn't been able to say no to gregarious, winsome Jo any more than Faith had. It was Jo who had convinced her it would be worthwhile to attend the auction today, to bid for one of the local men to help her clean up her run-down property. It had seemed like a good idea at the time, but in hindsight, she now decided she must have been clean out of her mind to have bid on a perfect stranger—one who had looked large and intimidating even from a distance.

Jax exited the stage, taking the stairs one slow step at a time, his gaze narrowed onto her and he frowned. The reluctance with which he moved to her side was palpable.

Now, as he approached her, *intimidated* didn't even begin to cover what she was feeling. At five feet ten inches in her bare feet—and three inches taller than that at the moment, thanks to her heels—Faith wasn't in any way diminutive. She was taller than most women and many men, but Jax towered over her.

Faith found it hard to believe that Jo had had the audacity to call him out by his given and middle names together, reminding her of the way a mother would scold an errant youngster climbing a tree. And right in front of the whole town, to boot. Jo and Jax must have a special relationship, because Faith had been shocked down to her shoes when Jax *had* turned around and returned to the platform just as Jo had asked.

Yet he was no wayward child. Far from it. If she had to guess, she'd put him a few years older than her own twenty-seven years. Thirty-ish. She judged him to be over two hundred pounds of raw muscle and a good six feet four inches tall, cartoonishly huge next to Jo's five-feet-nothing. He dwarfed the friendly redhead.

Unlike the guy who'd come before him, he hadn't even needed to flex for her—er—for the *crowd* to appreciate the strength of his broad shoulders and powerful biceps. Now in closer proximity, she inhaled the smell of him—all leather and raw man. Just the way he looked. The crazy thing was, that heady scent wasn't unpleasant. Quite the opposite, in fact.

If it weren't for the scar on his face, she'd have thought he'd walked right out of an advertisement for aftershave or something else meant to be rugged and manly. Though honestly, the ragged, puckered scar that slashed across the man's temple didn't bother her as much as the fact that he appeared to be glowering. Not at her, thankfully, but at a couple of sturdy cowboys standing together near the other side of the stage. The guy who'd been bid on first was there, his arm curved familiarly around his wife's waist. The other fellow, a big bear of a man whom Faith immediately dubbed *Grizzly Adams*, was grinning as if he'd triumphed in a race.

Jax's brothers, were Faith to guess. The family resemblance was striking in their similar strong features—the dark wavy hair and chiseled jaws.

Alexis gave Faith's shoulder an encouraging pat and turned back to the auction, where the next bachelor had broken into an impromptu round of "Home on the Range," presumably to impress the ladies with his vocal capabilities. Faith thought perhaps the guy should have chosen another talent to display. Singing in tune didn't appear to be part of his skill set. To Faith's ears, he sounded a bit like a crowing rooster, but she supposed it was the thought that counted. For some inexplicable reason the crowd was encouraging the poor bachelor, which only made him bellow all the louder.

She turned her attention to Jax. He was watching the guy on stage, but he didn't appear to care one way or another about the assault on his ears. She observed him quietly, hoping to discern what he might be thinking by the look on his face. She could read nothing in his expression. It wasn't empty so much as—*hard*. Frozen solid, like the frost in his eyes. His body language was equally as closed off, with his arms crossed over the bulk of his chest.

"So," she said, not at all certain how to start a conversation with him. "I brought a picnic basket full of goodies so we can share lunch together." She knew she was rambling but didn't seem to know how to stop. "I thought Jo's idea was a clever twist to the event, allowing everyone to participate in one way or another. Men, women, singles and married alike. Don't you think?"

He didn't respond, not even to acknowledge that she'd spoken to him. He hadn't even bothered to turn his head in her direction.

"Jax?" She touched his elbow to get his attention.

He turned, his piercing, chocolate-brown eyes shifting to hers and widening in surprise, as if he'd forgotten she was there.

Maybe he had.

"I—er—" she stammered. "Did you want to stay and watch the rest of the auction?"

Jax snorted. "Thank you, no. I am *so* done with this stupid event."

Faith smiled. "I thought you might be. I certainly wouldn't want to have to put myself up for display on the auction block, but I appreciate your sacrifice for the sake of the senior center building fund."

"Oh, believe me, I *felt* like a sacrifice. The lamb-to-the-slaughter kind." Jax grinned, his smile made slightly crooked by the tension created by his scar, which pulled the left side of his mouth higher than the right. It would have looked a bit like a grimace, except that his eyes were gleaming with amusement. "Thanks for rescuing me."

"My pleasure." Her cheeks warmed. She couldn't imagine why his words would make her blush. She swallowed and quickly recovered her composure. She pointed down the lawn. "I set my picnic basket under that oak tree over there. Are you hungry?"

A laugh that sounded a little bit like a growl emerged from deep in his chest. "I'm always hungry."

Well, duh. She should have guessed that. Put fur on the guy and he could probably pass for Bigfoot. Of course he was hungry.

"I hope I packed enough."

His right brow arched and the strained half grin returned.

She was already blushing, but now heat rushed to her face and spread to her cheeks like a wildfire. Had she just said those words out loud?

Open mouth, insert foot. Way to go, Faith. Insult the man ten seconds after meeting him.

She quickly tried to recover, feeling as if she were scrambling backward as she stammered her way through her sentence. "Oh, n-no. That's not what I intended to say. My words didn't come out right at *all*. I—I only meant—"

He held up one large work-calloused hand to stem the flow of her sputtering words. "It's okay, ma'am. Whatever you've brought will be just fine, I'm sure. I'm not a difficult man to please."

"Please call me Faith," she urged, brushing

her suddenly sweaty palms against the denim of her designer skinny jeans.

Acquiring new, more practical boot-cut jeans was on her priority list of things to do now that she was finally here in Serendipity. And as much as she loved her Jimmy Choos, her good pair of cowboy boots would have been much more sensible for the occasion. She was practically aerating the park grass with her three-inch spikes.

"Faith," he repeated, his rich, lyrical voice making her name sound like a musical note. "I'm Jax McKenna, and apparently I am at your service."

"It's nice to officially meet you, Jax." She held out her hand and he dwarfed it in his own. Again she had the impression of hard work and calluses, a complete contrast to her own lotion-softened, office-cubicle working hands.

That will change. Soon.

She'd spent the last few years working in accounting for a non-profit organization to save up the money for her horse sanctuary. Mere months from now she hoped and prayed that her palms would likewise carry the blisters of hard country labor. She could barely wait for that day, anticipating it like a child would Christmas morning. She was a city girl with a country heart.

"Here we are," she said, gesturing to a rather plain-looking brown wicker basket lingering next to the trunk of an oak, shaded from the glare of the sun by the old tree's branches. As she looked around at the other baskets dotting the lawn, she couldn't help but feel a little bit embarrassed. Her own meager offering looked so bare and ordinary next to the others. Many of the women had decorated their baskets with colorful plumes and ribbons. She wished she'd thought of that—especially because the man she'd be sharing a meal with looked as if he could use a few kindhearted gestures. But on the other hand, he didn't seem like the sort of man who'd really be comfortable with something dolled up and fancy. Maybe plain was best, after all.

Without speaking, Jax crouched over the basket, withdrawing a blue-checked plastic tablecloth that had been the best Faith could do under the circumstances. She'd arrived in Serendipity only two days ago and hadn't learned of the auction until the day prior.

How she'd come to bet on *this* particular tall, sturdy cowboy was a mystery even to her. It was nothing more than a gut feeling, but she'd learned over the years to follow those silent promptings.

Thankfully, the man with the rooster voice had stopped singing, but the crowd was still hooting and hollering in the background. Jax didn't seem to notice, nor, apparently, did he want to wait for the rest of the town to finish with the auction before he and Faith started on their picnic.

He spread the tablecloth across the grass and gestured for her to sit. Then he pulled out plates and silverware and popped the top of a cola can before offering it to her.

"Thanks," she said, dropping onto the far corner of the plastic and folding her legs under her. "Although I feel like I ought to be doing the serving," she said as he inspected the club sandwiches she'd made for the occasion. At least she'd used foot-long sub buns and loaded the sandwiches with meat, cheese and veggies. Dagwood would be proud of her creation.

Jax glanced up at her, and the unscarred side of his lips curled upward. Close to a smile, at any rate. Faith would take it.

"You paid for my time," he reminded her. "I figured now is as good a time as any to start working off my—" He paused and bent his head as he considered how best to finish the sentence.

"Community service?" she suggested, chuckling at the double meaning.

"Yeah. That." He wasn't laughing.

"I—uh—okay, right," she stammered. She didn't usually stutter like a schoolgirl with her first crush. If she didn't get a hold of her tongue soon, he would think he was working for an idiot.

His gaze had returned to the basket, giving Faith a modicum of reprieve. She took a deep, calming breath. There was no reason spending time with this man should visibly shake her, and the sooner she got comfortable around him, the better. After all, if he was as good with horses as Jo claimed, she hoped she might be able to convince him to stretch out his community service and continue working with her until her project was—if not finished, then a great deal closer than it was right now.

Then again, maybe he was expecting nothing more than to provide one day's labor. No one had really set the guidelines for what happened after the auction, or at least nothing that Faith had heard.

"There are canisters of potato salad and barbecue baked beans, as well," she added, relieved when her voice came out sounding normal. "I'm not much of a cook, but I made them myself. The beans are an old family recipe. Back home we called them Cowboy Beans." The thought struck her as funny and she chuckled.

"Well, that's fittin'." He pulled out the plastic container of beans and scooped a heaping portion onto each of their plates. "Where's home?"

He sounded genuinely interested, putting her more at ease. She leaned back on her hands. "I was born out east. Connecticut. I attended college in Wyoming. That's where I got interested in horses." It was also where she'd met…

She cut the thought off firmly, refusing to let her mind wander in that direction again. It still hurt to think about Keith and his son. She coughed, realizing Jax was speaking and she'd missed what he'd just said. "I'm sorry. My mind wandered for a second there. What did you say?"

His dark eyebrows lowered over stormy brown eyes. He assessed her, the working side of his lip curving into a frown. "Nothing important. Just that there's good horse country out in Wyoming. Potato salad?"

"Yes, please." She was relieved that he

didn't push her on what had caused her distraction. She wasn't ready to talk about Keith, or about his precious son.

They ate in silence for a while, each lost in thought. As the auction continued, more people moved to the green, milling around them, talking and laughing. Some even stopped to introduce themselves. Faith should have been happy to be so welcomed by her new community, but her empty chest echoed with the sounds.

Before she knew it, Jax had cleaned his plate—not once, but twice, leaving her glad she'd thought to pack extra. Jo Spencer had advised her on the eating habits of the Texas male, and Jax was no slouch in that department.

"If you don't mind me asking—why?" Jax's voice had a hard edge to it, and he didn't quite meet her gaze.

"Why?" she repeated, bracing herself. She wasn't ready for him to elaborate on his question, to have to explain why a city woman wanted to open up a mustang sanctuary in the country, but sometimes there was no way out but through.

"Yeah. Why?" He lifted his tan cowboy hat and brushed his forearm across his brow. "Why did you bid on me?"

Her heart skipped a beat. Why *had* she bid on him?

"You mean why did I bid in the auction in general, or why bid for you, specifically?"

He shrugged. "Both, I guess."

The truth was, he'd looked miserable up on the auction block, especially when there was hesitation from the crowd on bidding for him. She couldn't imagine why that was. Despite his scar, he was quite handsome, if a woman liked her men strong and rugged. Faith would have expected the town's single ladies to be shouting over each other in order to get a chance to spend time with this guy.

And yet there had been silence. The drop-of-a-pin kind.

Maybe it was too early in the game. Jax was only the second man to be auctioned, and the first bachelor. Perhaps the ladies were waiting to see who else was offering their services. Or maybe there was something about Jax that Faith didn't yet know about, such as that he was conceited or had a bad temper.

She hoped not, but she was about to find out—because Jax was frowning again.

"Look—I don't want your pity," he said, his voice husky.

"What? No."

"Are you seriously going to sit there and

tell me you didn't feel sorry for this scarred old monster? Because I won't believe you."

"I was standing at the back of the crowd. I couldn't even see your scar."

He shook his head. "That's even worse."

Now she was the one feeling insulted. "Why? You think I'm so shallow that I would want to bow out of our agreement just because of a gash on your face?"

He scoffed. "Wouldn't be the first time."

She heard the bitterness behind his words. Someone in his past had injured him deeply. The wound in his heart was deeper than the one on his face.

"Well, that's not me. I came here today looking for someone to help me with my ranch. I bought the Dennys' old place, and it will take a lot of labor to get it in working order. If you're going to pitch in, then I couldn't care less what you look like. Wear a paper bag over your face, if you like. It won't matter to me. I'll take all the help I can get."

His jaw lost its tightness at the welcome change of subject. He whistled softly.

"That place is pretty run-down. What do you plan to do with it?"

"I'm going to save wild mustangs." Her voice rose in pitch as enthusiasm for her life's dream engulfed her.

His gaze turned skeptical and his lips quirked. "Are you serious?"

Of course she was serious. Ever since she'd heard of the plight of wild mustangs as a child, she'd had it in her heart to take action, to make a difference. That's why she'd left the East Coast and picked a college in Wyoming. For a while, life had gotten in the way and she'd set aside her dreams. But after what happened with Keith—she refused to dwell on that part of her life—she'd started making legitimate plans to fulfill her goals, and now here she was, in Serendipity, a brand-new owner of a ranch, however derelict it was.

Baby steps.

"You doubt me?"

He leaned his back against the solid trunk of the oak and stretched out his legs, crossing them at the ankles, and giving her a once-over that sent chills down her spine.

His gaze lingered on her shoes.

"Forgive me if I'm a little bit skeptical. You're clearly a city girl. What do you know about ranching?"

The only reason she didn't punch him in the arm for his sarcasm—apart from not really knowing the man and how he'd react to that kind of attack—was that his words were lined with amusement. Hopefully not at her expense.

"All right. I'll admit I was born and raised in a metropolitan area and have never lived on a ranch. However, I have spent several years volunteering at a wild-horse sanctuary. I realize I'm on a learning curve here, but I have read a lot and my bachelor's degree is in business management with a minor in conservation and environmental science. I've done a lot of studying on the subject. Wyoming isn't tolerant of wild horses."

He snorted. "You've *read* about it? Like in a library? And you think a little piece of paper somehow makes you qualified to manage a horse farm? With wild mustangs, no less. Exactly how many wranglers do you intend to hire?"

She shook her head. She was afraid this subject might come up. "None. At least at first. I'm working to find like-minded donors to help me reach my vision, but until more funds come in, I can't afford to hire any help."

"You're doing this alone?"

"Well, not *all* alone, obviously. I have you, don't I? At least for a little while? I don't think we've talked about the length of your— *indenture*."

"I think most guys are going a month of weekends."

"That'll do. You can show me how to get the ranch up to scratch. I'm a fast learner."

"You're going to have to be, because fixing up the ranch won't be your only obstacle. Just how much experience do you have with mustangs? I've spent my whole life working with horses, and they still surprise me from time to time. Wild mustangs? That's a whole other thing."

"Yes, but they need my help." Her pulse quickened as adrenaline blasted through her and her spirit lifted. For a moment Jax's words and attitude had discouraged her, but then she remembered how many ways the Lord had come through for her. He'd guided her to Jax. She didn't believe in coincidences.

"You train horses, then?" She wanted specifics.

"Quarter horses for ranching and rodeo." His eyes gleamed with pride. It appeared they shared a love of horses. She just had to convince him she was serious in her intentions.

"I'd love to see your herd."

His gaze widened epically and Faith choked on her breath. Had she just invited herself over to his property? Heat flared to her cheeks.

To her surprise, he nodded. "Sure. Why

not? If you don't have any other plans this afternoon, we can head on over there after we've finished eating. Give you the opportunity to see a working ranch in action and get up close and personal with a real, live horse."

"Excuse me?" she huffed. "I've been around horses, thank you very much—and ranches, too. I worked at a ranch every summer while I was in college, and since I graduated, I've been volunteering weekends at Mustang Mission. I'm not the greenhorn you seem to think I am."

"Your shoes would suggest otherwise."

She chuckled. "Hey. I wasn't planning to go riding today. I'm new in town. I had to guess at the dress code. For all I knew this auction would be a black-tie event. Were we in a larger metropolitan area it probably would have been tuxes and cocktail dresses."

A rich, deep laugh rumbled through his chest. "In Serendipity, honey, we have exactly two dress codes. Go-to-church clothes and everything else. If you ever have a doubt, dress casual."

He tipped his hat and her heart purred. This was where she wanted to be. In the country, with real horses, real cowboys and a real chance to make a difference. Not back home where no one—except her friends at Mustang Mission—seemed to understand what she wanted to achieve.

This was *home*. She felt it in every fiber of her being.

Now she just had to convince her new neighbors—and the possibly hostile cattle community—that she and her mustangs belonged there.

Chapter Two

Jax's phone trilled. He slipped it out of the plain black leather case he wore on his belt, glanced at the number and scowled.

Susie.

"Now why would she...?" The rest of his sentence trailed off into puzzled silence. He grimaced. His ex-wife was the last person he wanted to talk to, especially today. Faith had somehow, although he had no idea how, gotten him out of his own head for a while. He'd actually been enjoying himself for a change, and that had happened far too little in his life in the nine months since Susie left him.

Count on Susie to dump ice water on his good mood. Without even answering the phone, he sensed she was about to completely ruin what up until now had been a perfectly good day.

It just figured.

He cupped his hand over the receiver and flashed Faith an apologetic shrug.

"Excuse me just a moment, will you, Faith? I'd better take this. It's my ex-wife on the line."

"Of course," she said with an encouraging smile. "Take all the time you need."

He strode a few steps away from Faith and held the phone to his ear, trying not to grit his teeth when he spoke.

"Did you need something?" Jax didn't bother with pleasantries. He couldn't imagine what she wanted. He'd already done what he could for her. He hadn't contested the divorce, hadn't protested the way she'd taken almost everything of value from the house when she left, hadn't even argued over the amount of money she'd taken from their shared accounts—though he remained deeply grateful that the ranch's accounts were separate and that she hadn't been able to access them. She'd drained away everything she could from him, including his confidence and pride, until the love he'd once felt for her had withered into dust. He had nothing left to give her.

So why was she contacting him now?

"Are you at the house?"

"No, I'm not." He started to tell her he was

at the auction but then cut his words short. His shoulders tightened with strain and his gut squeezed so forcefully he could barely breathe. He didn't have to answer to her, not about his whereabouts or any other part of his life.

Besides, Susie didn't even live in Serendipity anymore. She despised the small town in which she'd been born and raised. She probably didn't even know about the auction, seeing as it was the first—and Jax hoped *only*—one ever.

"Why are you asking? Are you in town? Do you need to see me for something?" Had there been some kind of legal hang-up? He hoped not. He'd thought the divorce was a done deal.

"Go home. Now."

"What?" Jax asked, his voice a low rumble. He didn't care for the way she was ordering him around.

"Just go." She sounded a little desperate.

"Wait—" Heat flared through him in a flash of foreboding and he muttered something unintelligible under his breath. "Susie? Susie?"

Dead air met his ear and he glanced at the face of his phone. She'd hung up on him. Tried to boss him around and then hung up on him. He growled and pressed the redial button but the call went straight to voice mail.

"Are you okay?" Faith asked when he returned to the picnic blanket and slumped to his knees, bracing his hands on his thighs and breathing raggedly. Her gaze looked troubled, though why she should care was beyond him.

He lifted his hat by the crown and shoved his fingers through his thick, unmanageable hair, then replaced it and pulled the brim low over his eyes to shadow his scar.

"Yeah," he answered with a clipped nod. His pulse was still thundering and the notion that something was amiss continued to hover over him like a storm cloud. "Well, no. Not really. To tell you the truth, I'm not sure."

She remained silent while Jax worked through his thoughts, her gaze more compassionate than curious. He appreciated that she didn't try to push him to speak before he was ready.

Go home. Now.

He thought about just ignoring Susie's words and going back to his very pleasant picnic, but there was something off in her tone. Desperate. A sharp edge in his gut nagged at him, obliging him to change his plans.

"I hate to rush you, but would you mind if we pack up our picnic and take off now?"

"Sure thing," she said, reaching for the plastic lids to cover the leftover potato salad and baked beans. "Not a problem. I hope everything is okay."

"Thanks." He was already haphazardly folding the checked tablecloth and stuffing it into the picnic basket along with the plates and napkins Faith handed to him. His ex-wife's words echoed through him, rattling his cage.

He frowned. He wouldn't give her the gratification of knowing how rough these months had been. He wasn't certain he could face her now, but that's what she must have meant—that she was waiting for him at the house. But if she had something to tell him, why couldn't she have just said it over the phone?

Faith touched his forearm. When he turned and met her gaze, she was looking at him expectantly. Clearly, she'd asked him a question and he hadn't responded.

It wasn't the first time he'd found himself in this position. He floundered through the options but came up with too many possibilities for him to narrow down. What had she asked him about?

The auction? The picnic? His ex?

He generally tried to stay on the offensive when it came to his hearing deficiency. After his accident he'd lost nearly 100 percent of his hearing in his left ear. He'd become proficient at lipreading and responding to subtle body-language cues. Most of the time it was enough to get by, although he hated that he occasionally gave the wrong answer or said something that didn't fit in the conversation.

It was an embarrassing disability and one he didn't like to talk about. Few in town even knew about it.

His family—his mom and his two brothers, Nick and Slade—were patient with him, understanding his dilemma. He'd become kind of a recluse after the accident—after Susie left. He emerged only for Sunday services at church and the occasional necessary trip to town for supplies. He was quick to leave church right afterward, not staying around to socialize, and he'd quit stopping in at Cup O' Jo's Café to catch up on the news.

"I'm sorry, what?" he asked Faith after an extended pause, smiling apologetically and hoping she wouldn't catch on to his disability. It was bad enough having hearing loss without having to talk about it. Though he'd kept his condition mostly secret, he knew that deafness—even only partial deafness—made many folks uneasy.

"I asked if you'd rather that I make my

visit to your ranch another day. It sounds like you've got your hands full right now."

He immediately shook his head. "No. Please. I'm anxious to show you my herd."

He did want to show her his prize-winning horses, but at the moment he just felt the overwhelming need for backup in case Susie was there. Better not to be alone in that case. Having someone else around might keep her from making a scene. He could ask one of his brothers, but there was no sense interrupting their day when Jax and Faith had already made plans together.

Besides, it was probably nothing.

"Okay, then. I'll come with you," she said, her voice just a hair too high and bright. "If you don't mind my asking, though—why the sudden hurry?"

"My ex-wife just called. Said I needed to hurry home. Honestly, I don't know what she's up to, but I figured I'd better find out."

"I see." Faith nodded, but thankfully didn't ask any more probing questions to which he didn't have any answers.

They loaded the picnic basket in the bed of Jax's truck and drove back toward his ranch. He clenched his fists on the steering wheel and forced himself to breathe evenly, concentrating on tamping back the fury burning in his chest. He thought he was over feeling *anything* when it came to Susie. He'd been on his knees dozens of times praying he could forgive her for the hurt she'd caused him.

Apparently, he hadn't prayed hard enough.

He barely registered it when he turned into the long gravel driveway that housed the Circle M ranch. His mother, Alice, a recent widow, lived in the main ranch house, while Jax and Nick held separate residences on the land, smaller cabins that better fit their bachelor status. Slade had moved to the Beckett ranch next door when he'd married Laney.

He pulled up before his cabin, expecting to see Susie's red AWD parked in front, or worse yet, a courier with more unpleasant papers to sign. He scanned the area for an unfamiliar vehicle but didn't find one. He'd seen a truck kicking up dust on the road that led to the Circle M, but it hadn't occurred to him that it might be Susie. He'd seen only the back of the relatively new blue pickup, but now that he thought about it, it had appeared to be exceeding the speed limit on its way out of town.

Great. What was Susie up to, anyway? He was going to be good and angry if she'd pulled him away from the picnic and the nicest day he'd had in—well, he couldn't remember how long—for no good reason.

Oh, who was he kidding? He was *good and angry* now.

He hopped out of the cab and hurried around to open up the door for Faith. It wasn't just that his mama had taught him to be a gentleman. With those ridiculously high heels she was wearing, she was bound to take a digger if she tried to get down by herself. He was having a hard enough day without becoming responsible for the impractically dressed woman twisting her ankle.

She smiled up at him gratefully as he grasped her tiny waist and lifted her from the cab. She reached for his shoulders to maintain her balance, and his hands lingered on her waist.

Their eyes met and held, and her cheeks turned a pretty shade of rose before she cleared her throat and stepped away from him, her gaze shifting from his face to the front of his cabin.

"What a lovely place," she complimented. "Your cabin looks like it belongs in a magazine."

He cringed inwardly. It only now occurred to him that he might not want to invite her inside. He couldn't remember if he'd picked up his laundry or not, and he had a bad habit of leaving his soiled socks where he shed them, not to mention a week's worth of dirty dishes he had piled in the sink. He didn't have a dishwasher and usually got to washing the dishes only when he didn't have anything left to eat on.

He was busy formulating a reasonable explanation for the mess inside when Faith's eyes widened and her mouth made a perfect O. And she hadn't even seen his dirty laundry yet.

"Jax?" She whispered his name like a question, her voice sounding like sandpaper, not at all the sweet, high, smooth timbre she'd used earlier in the day.

The warning in her tone sent a ripple of apprehension down his spine. Slowly he turned, afraid to see what had so obviously shaken her. He wouldn't put anything past Susie at this point.

Oh, dear Lord, no.

His gut clenched as he gasped for air and a proverbial sideswipe to his jaw sent him reeling.

No. It couldn't be. It could. Not. Be.

Jax blinked and scrubbed a hand down his face.

Were his eyes deceiving him?

Impossible.

Even if he was blind as a bat, and even though his hearing was half what it used to be, there was no mistaking the sound of distinctive, distraught mewling coming from two tiny swaddled infants, bundled into their car seats and blocking the front door of his cabin.

Babies?

He took the steps two at a time and crouched before the baby on his left, gently adjusting the pink blanket covering her and making what he hoped were calming shushing noises. His expertise was horses. He knew zero about babies.

She was incredibly tiny next to his large palm. So vulnerable. So defenseless. He swallowed hard.

How long had they been here, *alone*, where any number of ills could befall them?

The—*babies*.

Fury roared and blazed like a wildfire in his chest. Susie had left two helpless infants on his front porch? She was going to answer for this. She'd always been irresponsible and often acted with poor judgment, but this went far beyond the pale even for her.

"Jax?" Faith asked again, her voice faltering. She knelt before the other baby, presumably also a girl, given the identical pink blanket tucked around her, and gently rocked the seat to calm the infant. "Are these…?"

"I don't—I'm not—" Jax stammered, his head spinning. He considered himself calm and rational. His emotions rarely got the better of him. But right now he was fighting with every ounce of his courage against succumbing to the conflicting feelings pelting him—a lone unarmed man against an army of men with razor-sharp swords and blistering bows and arrows.

Shock. Surprise. Anger. Betrayal. Guilt. Pain.

Wonder.

Were these…? Could it be that these precious little pieces of humanity were…?

His heart welled and tears pricked at the corners of his eyes. He couldn't lose it now. He just couldn't.

He stood abruptly, and the baby at his feet protested with a wail. She had a nice, healthy pair of lungs on her, and Jax winced, then crouched back down and rocked the car seat as Faith was doing.

Where was Susie? How could she possibly have just *left* these babies behind without an explanation? He had a million questions to ask her, and he wanted to tell her exactly

what he thought of her inconceivably self-
ish behavior. He'd never actually throttle a
woman, even Susie, but the thought did cross
his mind, to shake a little sense into her.

How could she?

How could she keep such an enormous
secret from him? If these were, in fact, his
daughters...

She'd kept his *children* from him, kept him
from knowing they even existed. They were
probably no more than a month old—not that
he could guess with any accuracy. She should
have told him she was pregnant as soon as she
knew she was pregnant. He should have been
there when the babies were born.

He was their father. He had rights. Responsibilities. Privileges.

How *dare* she?

He fished out his phone and punched Susie's
number again, but not surprisingly, it went
straight to voice mail. Again. She was avoiding him, as well she might, considering what
she'd just done. Was she seriously just dump-
ing a couple of babies on his doorstep and
running away?

No. Not just a couple of babies.

His babies.

He didn't know how he knew they were
his children. Given Susie's actions during the

past year, their paternity might well be called into question, but his heart and his gut were telling him there was no doubt that he was the babies' father. And not just because Susie had dumped them on his doorstep.

Overcoming every other emotion he was feeling, even the most heated ones, amazement and wonder and love warmed his chest, swirling and curling around and filling his heart full to the brim.

He was astounded by how instantly those feelings appeared and how strong they were. He'd woken up this morning a man who had been living practically like a hermit, deliberately isolating himself, mucking through the mire of his own despair.

Alone.

And now—

Now he was a *father*.

"Should we take them inside, do you think?" Faith asked hesitantly.

"What? Yes." He'd nearly forgotten Faith was there, but he was grateful she was. He wasn't even remotely capable of dealing with this crisis on his own, and her question proved it. He didn't know what to do with one baby, never mind two.

Of course he needed to take the infants inside the cabin, and then…

What next?

He didn't know the first thing about infants. Not what they ate, though presumably it was milk of some kind. Not how to get them to sleep, or even where they should sleep. It wasn't as if he had a crib in his spare room. He didn't even know how to change a diaper.

Faith stood and touched his shoulder. "You look lost."

And frightened.

She didn't say it, but they both knew it.

He met her empathetic hazel eyes and groaned. "I feel lost. Like on-another-planet lost. I don't have a clue what I should do next. This is so beyond my realm of experience— almost beyond reality, actually."

She nodded. "I can't even imagine what you're going through. It's not every day a man learns he's a father when his babies show up at his door. Let's get these two little darlings in out of the heat and tend to their immediate needs, and then we can make a plan."

She'd said *we* as if it were just a given that she'd be part of—whatever this was. Her voice teemed with compassion and confidence. He was grateful that she'd come to Serendipity and chosen it to be her home. He was glad he'd met her. It was no accident that she'd bid on him today.

He knew in his heart that as crazy as this whole thing was, the Lord was watching over him. Faith's presence proved it. Even though she hadn't known him for more than a few hours, she offered her support and was willing to stay with him—with *them*. He *needed* her here.

He unlocked the door to his cabin, and Faith held the screen door for him as he grabbed the handles of both of the car seats and carefully transferred the children—*his* children—indoors. He scanned the area for the best place to put the car seats and settled on the carpet between the front of the couch and the coffee table.

Faith followed with a diaper bag in her hand—which, in the shock and devastation of the moment, had escaped Jax's notice. He supposed he should be grateful Susie had left him a modicum of supplies, but he was too angry to give her even that. He hoped she'd left a note giving him some idea of her state of mind—and the children's names would be nice, at the very least.

He turned his attention to one of the babies while Faith took care of the other. It took him a moment to figure out the lock system on the car seat, and by the time he was ready to lift the infant out, Faith already had hers tucked

safely in the crook of her arm and was smiling and making delightful cooing noises to
the contented infant.

He'd finally managed to unhook the straps
but hesitated in removing the tiny little human
being from the seat. He didn't know what he
was doing. What if he accidentally hurt her?

"Support her neck with one hand and
slide the other one behind her back," Faith
instructed, as if she knew what he'd been
thinking.

"Right." He cleared his throat and rubbed
a hand down his jaw. This wasn't going to
get any easier by waiting, and unlike the infant Faith held, his baby girl was starting to
fuss again.

He held his breath and slid his hand underneath her, trying to be gentle but feeling like
a clumsy giant. His daughter was so tiny he
could easily support her neck and back with
one hand, but he didn't take any chances. He
followed Faith's directions to the letter.

The baby was incredibly fragile, weighing
next to nothing. He held her out in front of
him and swallowed hard around the lump of
emotion in his throat.

"She's crying and yours isn't," he said, his
voice scratchy. "What am I doing wrong?"

Faith chuckled. "You're doing fine. Don't

worry about the fussing. Babies do that. She's just communicating with you. Put her up against your shoulder and pat her back. She's likely hungry or wet or both. The first thing we should do is see about getting these sweethearts changed into dry diapers and then get them some bottles of formula to warm and fill their little bellies." She sat down on the sofa and kissed her baby's forehead. "Let's see what we've got here."

Jax adjusted the baby he was holding to his shoulder, and to his surprise, she immediately calmed down. He watched Faith remove the contents of the stylish red diaper bag. She placed everything she found on the coffee table—a stack of diapers, a box of wet wipes, four plastic bottles and a couple of yellow cans bearing a brand name Jax didn't recognize. He couldn't even begin to guess what was inside. A couple of yellow T-shirts with snaps on the bottom.

"Diapers first, then formula." Faith spread a blanket on the floor and laid her baby down, gesturing for Jax to do the same.

"What's formula?" Jax asked, following Faith's lead. He carefully unwrapped the blankets swaddled around his infant and removed the wet diaper.

"It's like milk, only it's specifically made for babies' sensitive stomachs."

"I don't have any formula." Jax gently lifted the baby's legs and slid a diaper underneath her. He started to tape the tabs only to realize the diaper was backward.

Tabs in back, cartoon picture in front.

Good thing he was a fast learner.

"Yes, you do." Faith nodded toward the yellow cans. "But that stash won't last very long, especially with two little ones. You'll have to get to the store soon."

Like *today*. And not just for formula, but for all the other things two babies would need.

Most people had nine months to plan their baby's arrival. He hadn't had a single second. And with the whole town wrapped up for the weekend with the special event, he wouldn't be able to visit Sam's Grocery until Monday. He hoped he could make it that long. When he had the opportunity, he'd call Slade and Laney and see if they had anything he could use.

Satisfied that he had his daughter's diaper fastened—if not perfectly then at least adequately—he lifted her back into his arms. Faith likewise picked up her infant, but then also somehow managed to balance two bottles and a can of formula in her other arm. Talented woman.

"Kitchen?"

"Through the door on the left," he said, nodding toward the small space that served him as a kitchen.

"Can I help?" he asked her, not knowing how much assistance he could actually provide.

"No need." She chuckled.

She was obviously going to set up the bottles for the infants, though Jax had no clue what that entailed, much less how she was going to manage with only one free hand. He looked around, wondering what he ought to do next and wishing babies came with a written how-to manual.

Well, okay, maybe not a *manual*. He wasn't much on reading directions. But a bulleted list, at least.

He stared down at the tiny slip of humanity nestled in the crook of his arm, smacking noisily on her little fist that she'd caught in her mouth, and felt yet another overwhelming surge of joy and amazement. His throat closed around the emotion, clogging his breath.

His baby. Sweet…

His mind sluggishly wrapped around his biggest problem yet. He hadn't seen a note in the paraphernalia Faith had emptied from the diaper bag.

"What's your name, little darlin'?"

Her arms laden with the second twin and trying to balance two warm bottles, Faith froze in the doorway, her gaze checked on the large man with the tiny infant enfolded in his muscular arms.

He'd spoken aloud. And he was right.

How was he supposed to deal with *that* issue? He could hardly care for the twins without names. Susie wasn't answering her phone and there didn't appear to be a note anywhere.

She shook her head and scoffed softly. This whole thing was messed up on so many levels that she couldn't even begin to catalog them. It was surreal.

They couldn't continue to refer to the two babies as *your baby* and *my baby* based on which infant they were holding, first because they were both his children and second because Faith would be leaving soon, or at least as soon as they could find someone else to assist him. There was no question that he'd need round-the-clock help, at least for the first few days.

Jax pulled out his phone and from the expression on his face, she could tell that he'd dialed Susie once again, but of course the senseless woman wasn't answering. Not that Faith expected her to. What woman in her right mind would drop her babies on someone's front step, even if that someone was the unsuspecting father? She was clearly immature and running away from her responsibilities. It was highly unlikely she'd offer Jax any kind of assistance now.

Faith coughed to let Jax know she was standing there, but he didn't acknowledge her. He didn't even look up. He was entirely focused on the baby in his arms.

He seemed to notice her only when she entered the living room and sat down on the couch across from his easy chair. She handed him a bottle and smiled encouragingly. With more actions than words, she showed him how to hold and angle the bottle for the precious little one in his arms. The baby took right to it, although Jax appeared a little self-conscious.

She leaned back into the middle cushion of the plush chocolate-colored couch and encouraged her baby—or rather, not *her* baby, but the infant she was holding—to root for the bottle. She was as hungry as her sister, and in moments the room was silent except for the sound of contented gurgling.

"I've got so many problems I don't know where to start. For one thing, I can't tell them apart," Jax admitted, his lips tightening into a thin, straight line. "And even if I could, Susie didn't leave a note to tell me what to call them. She could have at least pinned a name on them or something."

Faith looked from one baby to the other. Jax was right. The children looked exactly the same, from their scrunched-up expressions as they held the bottles to their chocolate-brown eyes. They were even dressed alike.

"You're right," she agreed. "That's a complication, but we'll figure it out. We don't know if they are identical or fraternal twins, but at this point in the game they are unquestionably going to be hard to tell one from the other. We need to look for some kind of defining features, something that sets the two apart."

He frowned and studied the infant in his arms, who was noisily enjoying her late lunch. "Like what?"

"I don't know. Let's compare. They both have the same thick tufts of brown hair."

Just like their daddy.

"Your baby's hair seems slightly curlier, but that could change after they've had a bath."

Jax's face paled and he made a choking sound. "A bath?"

She chuckled at his insecurity. He seemed like a take-charge kind of man, and yet a baby—two babies—left him helpless. It would be kind of cute, were it not so serious.

"With water," she teased. "Don't worry, we'll get there. I'm sure somebody can show you how it's done. Your mom has probably given babies a bath or two in her time."

"No doubt," he said, the corner of his mouth stretching up. "And I imagine my brothers and I were more trouble than these little girls are going to be."

Faith chuckled, imagining three rough-and-tumble boys in the bathtub. Jax's mother must have had a stern hand to have kept them in line.

"Maybe one of them has a birthmark," he suggested, bringing Faith's mind back to the present.

"How about dimples?" She'd known identical twins in high school, and that was how she'd been able to tell them apart, especially at first.

"Great idea. My baby has them. Both cheeks and a big one on her little chin."

"There you go, then." She nodded toward the baby in her arms. "This little sweetheart doesn't."

"One problem solved." Jax groaned. "But being able to tell them apart isn't going to help me if I don't know their names. I can't believe Susie did this to them."

Faith's heart swelled into her throat, and she could barely breathe around it. He wasn't thinking of the inconvenience to himself as much as the well-being of his babies. As for Faith, she couldn't believe Jax's ex-wife could do that to *him*. Maybe it was a good thing this Susie character had decided to leave the sweet little babies with Jax. At least he was mature and responsible. He'd take care of them. A woman who'd just leave her helpless babies on a doorstep in the Texas heat didn't even deserve to be called a mother.

"Thing One and Thing Two?" She spoke blithely, hoping somehow to lighten his very heavy load.

The other corner of his lips rose like the first, but his expression still looked strained, especially around his scar. "That would be one solution."

"I'm sorry, I really shouldn't be making so light of it," Faith continued. "It's pretty heavy stuff. I'm still trying to wrap my mind around Susie's actions. I can't believe a mother would up and abandon the babies the way she did. You have so little to go on, and it's not just baby supplies that you're lacking. You don't have a clue about what names might be on their birth certificates."

Jax scowled. "I don't even know if *I'm* listed on the birth certificates."

Probably not.

Given the circumstances, Faith doubted the woman would have officially acknowledged Jax's paternity until it suited her purposes, but she didn't tell him so. "You'll have to investigate that. I'm sure there are legal ways you can establish your paternity, whether your name is listed on the birth certificate or not. But in the meantime, I suggest you come up with nicknames for your daughters. You have to call them something."

The crease between his eyes deepened. "Like what?"

She shrugged. "I don't know. You could use family names. Maybe your grandmothers'?"

His jaw worked as he thought it over. "I like the idea of naming them after Granny Jane and Grandma Victoria, and if I'd had any say in it—on what went on their birth certificates—I might have suggested just those names. But if I name them Jane and Victoria, don't you think that might confuse them later when they realize the names on their birth certificates don't match what I've always called them?"

That was true enough. She nodded.

"I can probably explain a nickname as just a pet name I came up with, though that's not a conversation I ever want to have to have. I can't believe this. It's imperative that I speak to Susie again, and the sooner, the better. I'm sure that's why she's not picking up her phone. She's going to avoid me for as long as possible."

He growled in frustration. The baby he was holding squeaked and flapped her arms in distress, and Jax softened his tone. "It's okay, sweetheart. Daddy's here."

Faith's heart welled again. Everything Jax did with the babies seemed to have that effect on her.

He cringed and sent her a pleading glance. "Help me out here, Faith. I want to think of something soft and feminine but I'm at a complete loss. Sweetheart and Little Darlin' just aren't going to cut it, and I'm just not good at stuff like this."

This was new territory for Faith as well, but she didn't say so.

"Flowers?" Faith suggested tentatively. "Or colors?"

"How do you mean?"

"Marigold and you could call her Mary?"

His brow creased. Given the angle of his scar, she couldn't tell if he was amused or cringing.

"Daffodil and we could call her Daffy?"

A chuckle rumbled through his chest.

It was amusement, then. He was a hard man to read. She'd have to remember what his smile looked like.

She admired someone who could laugh in the face of adversity, and Jax was taking this remarkably well. She suspected most people would have fallen completely apart.

Her, for example. She would have lost it and would have been useless to anyone. She knew she would have. Unlike Jax, who was working through the stress and holding himself together, Faith was more inclined toward outright panic.

Even though she hadn't known him for more than a handful of hours, she already perceived that the infants were blessed to have a father like Jax. It was clear he'd take good care of them. They were so sweet and delicate, and oh so vulnerable, but they had someone to protect them.

Jax.

And he was right. They did deserve graceful names that befitted how precious and lovely they already were to him.

Suddenly an idea came to her. "Hey, I know. How about Rose and Violet?"

"Great idea. I like it." He sat back in the chair, and Faith could almost palpably feel relief rolling off his broad shoulders. "Flowers and colors. Really clever, Faith."

They shared a few minutes of silence, both attending to the needs of the twin in their arms. Faith's mind was spinning, organizing and prioritizing many of the details she was sure Jax had yet to consider. She didn't want to burden him further, but she couldn't even think about leaving until he'd made a few more decisions, and night was rapidly closing in.

"Do you have someone you can call to help you out tonight? A sister? Your mother?"

"No sisters, unfortunately. Only my two big-lug brothers. I do have a sister-in-law, Slade's wife, Laney, whom I could call in a pinch, I imagine. But I hate to burden her with this. She has a toddler of her own to care for, not to mention being about ready to pop with her next kid. Due in a couple of weeks, I think."

Faith chuckled. "Then you're right. Laney probably needs all the sleep she can get—though she might be able to stock you up on some baby supplies, if she's already got her nursery ready. And your mom?"

"Yes, maybe," he said, but he didn't sound too sure of himself. "She lives in the big ranch house we passed on our way in. She's all alone up there, and she definitely knows everything there is to know about baby care. It's just that—" He paused and shook his head.

Faith transferred her baby—little *Rose*—to her shoulder and gently patted the bubbles out while she waited for Jax to finish his sentence.

"My dad died about a year ago and she hasn't been the same since."

"Oh, that's too bad. I'm so sorry for your loss. How long were they together?"

"Forty-eight years."

Faith's breath escaped in a low gasp. "I can't imagine how difficult that must be for her."

Jax nodded. "She used to be bubbly and upbeat, the first in line at social events." Mimicking Faith's movements, he brought Violet to his shoulder and tapped lightly on her back. "But since Dad passed away, she's mostly just kept to herself. I hate to burden her with—"

"Her granddaughters?" Faith finished for him. Excitement welled in her chest as the idea expanded. "Jax, this might be a blessing in disguise. I—I mean, more than just that you've discovered you have two lovely infants," she stammered. "That's a blessing in itself, of course. But these precious babies might be just what your mother needs—a reason to hope and a way to feel like she matters again."

"She matters to my brothers and me."

"Yes, but you're grown men now with lives of your own. You don't need her the ways a baby would. Much less *two* babies."

"You know what? I see your point. She brightens up every time she holds her little grandson, Brody. I'll call her and see what she thinks."

Not having anywhere else to put her, Faith laid the now-sleeping Rose back into her car seat and took Violet from Jax's arms. "I'll rock Violet to sleep. You call your mom."

He flashed her a grateful half smile and reached for his phone. From what Faith gleaned from Jax's side of the conversation, his mother was in turn angry and then exhilarated. Pretty much the emotions they'd all experienced today.

"She's on her way," he said after he ended the call. "I haven't heard that kind of energy in her voice since—well, it's been a long time. I think you're right about this being a blessing for her. I'll tell you one thing, though. I sure wouldn't want to be Susie if my mom gets a hold of her. I've never heard her so angry."

"I imagine she'll have to stand in line where Susie is concerned."

"Isn't that the truth?"

Faith was glad for Jax that he had people who loved him enough to defend him, but it made her ache with loneliness. Mostly she was fine on her own, but there were moments where being alone segued into being *lonely*, and that was not the same thing at all.

This was one of those moments.

"I'm sorry I didn't have the chance to show you my horses today. That was the whole reason you came over, and then you got pulled into this drama. I really apologize for this. I was looking forward to showing off some of my training methods."

"It's not necessary to apologize. I'm glad I could be here for you. And I can see your horses and your training methods another time," she assured him. "You have far more important things to do right now than worry about my interests. That said, since your mom is on her way, I think I'll just skip out for now."

"But I drove you here."

"The community green isn't that far away, and I don't mind the walk."

"I'd really like to introduce you to my mother."

"I'd enjoy that, as well. But not today, I don't think. Grandma is going to want to focus all her attention on loving up your babies. I'd just be in the way."

Jax started to protest but Faith held up her hand.

It was time for her to make her exit, to let the new family adjust to being together.

And Faith? She would go home to an empty house.

Chapter Three

Jax was still marveling at the way his mother's countenance had sparked upon seeing her grandbabies. Faith had been right on every count. His mom had burst on the scene in a flurry of motion and energy the likes of which he hadn't seen in the past year, and had promptly taken over, calling a family meeting to inform everyone about the afternoon's events.

Though Jax was close to his brothers, it wouldn't have occurred to him to bring his whole family up to speed on the situation on the very first night. He trusted that his mom knew exactly what she was doing, and she had.

Not only that, she knew everything that the babies needed, and the when and how and why. She'd mentioned something about a schedule but Jax didn't see any real pattern to the babies' activities. Jax was picturing spreadsheets, but he was fairly certain he was off on that point.

His mother had sent Slade to fetch a bassinet from her spare room—the same one she'd used with Jax and his brothers when they were infants. He was grateful beyond all measure that Mom was too sentimental to throw those old baby things away, or he might have been in real trouble trying to find the twins a place to sleep.

Not that they slept much. Jax spent the weekend at his mother's house so she could share in caring for the infants, but he still felt as if he spent most of his time pacing up and down the hallway trying to comfort one baby or the other.

Monday morning he and his mother visited Emerson's Hardware and Sam's Grocery for infant paraphernalia. Jax was quickly learning that babies required a *lot* of stuff.

Cribs, a stroller, a changing table and a little plastic tub that fit in the kitchen sink so he could give his children baths. Then there were the clothes—the part about which his mother was most excited. Pink, pink and more pink. Ruffles and bows galore.

And as if that weren't enough, there were

the recurring needs—diapers, wipes and formula. Baby powder and baby shampoo. Jax's pocketbook was taking almost as much of a hit as his heart was.

But he'd been visited by several friends and neighbors who'd heard about his dilemma through Jo. He was grateful for their donations of baby items and even more for their emotional and spiritual support.

There was still no word from Susie, despite the fact that he'd left her countless messages. He was beginning to wonder if she was even more unstable than he'd originally believed her to be. Even before she'd abandoned her own children, her lifestyle had been less than stellar, which concerned Jax in regard to the health of his girls. One of his first stops on Monday had been to Dr. Delia. Thankfully, the twins appeared to be well and thriving.

If Susie *had* disappeared for good, Jax was legally at ground zero. He didn't even know where the babies had been born, never mind what hospital. It would take him some serious digging to find what he needed to lay claim to his children.

Even with the added hassle, he was beginning to believe it was just as well that Susie was gone. The fact that she had clearly abandoned the girls would help him in court, if it came to that. Now that he knew about his little darlin's, there was no way he would give up his custody of them, even if he had to fight Susie tooth and nail every step of the way. His daughters needed the kind of love and stability Susie clearly couldn't offer them right now. Even feeling as queasy-in-the-stomach overwhelmed as he did right now, he knew that with his family's help, he could provide everything his children needed.

Somehow, Lord help him, he would.

After setting up the cribs in his spare room that had been hastily converted into a nursery, his mom offered—no, *insisted*—that he take a break and go visit Faith. Jax and his mom had used caring for the babies together to mend some of the emotional stitching that had unraveled when his father had died and then when he'd had his accident.

They'd grown apart and Jax hadn't even realized it. It was only when they were speaking again that he realized how much he'd missed talking to his mom.

He'd told her how much he'd enjoyed the picnic with Faith, and a mischievous gleam immediately appeared in her eyes. And then she'd practically pushed him out the door, assuring him she had everything under control and he should get out and enjoy the sunshine.

Right. The sunshine.

Nothing would come of her overt attempt at matchmaking, but it was nice to see her smiling again. Besides, he owed Faith his time and labor. She had purchased him at the auction, after all, and for far more money than he was worth.

Jax knew the Dennys' spread hadn't been kept up over the past couple of years, but he never imagined the sorry state of the ranch he encountered as he drove up and parked in front of Faith's new home. Rotted shutters hung half off the hinges, and the screens covering the windows were torn through. It looked as though some animal or another had made use of the ranch house while the Dennys were elsewhere. The house needed a fresh coat of paint and new shingles on the roof. The wraparound deck was weatherworn and needed varnishing, and the flower beds in front were overgrown with weeds.

And that was to say nothing of the outbuildings and land around the house. He guessed the barn must have been red once, but now it was a muted orange color. The fences that were supposed to contain the corral and what he could see of the pasture land were in dire need of repair. The hay field was so overgrown it would take a season, maybe two, to set it right, and that was assuming Faith owned the appropriate farm equipment, which he highly doubted.

He wasn't even sure she had the right shoes.

It took him less than a minute of perusal before he knew that, on his own, his labor wouldn't be nearly enough for Faith to get this place into shape as quickly as she wanted. A community workday might be in order, and soon. She'd soon find her neighbors in Serendipity were generous with their time and talents.

One thing was certain—the property was in no way ready to host horses, especially wild ones.

He approached the front door, careful to avoid the rickety step, and rang the bell. When that yielded nothing, he knocked twice. When she still didn't answer, he decided to have a better look around the place. Faith's enormous, beat-up black SUV was parked in front of the house, so presumably she was around here somewhere. Searching for her was the perfect excuse—er—*opportunity* to take a closer look at the barn and surrounding countryside.

Get the lay of the land, so to speak.

Babies might not need spreadsheets, but it looked as if Faith's ranch was going to take a lot of them. This was a huge, huge project. He suspected she had no idea how big.

It didn't take him long to locate Faith. He called her name as he circled the barn, and she popped her head up from behind a wall of hay bales. She'd tied her platinum-blond hair into a loose bun held together with what looked like a pencil. Wisps had broken free to frame her exertion-reddened face. She wiped her elbow across her brow and smiled.

"What are you doing here?" Her question might have sounded abrupt but instead held a tone of pleasant surprise.

He saluted sloppily. "Jax McKenna, reporting for duty, ma'am."

She shook her head. "Oh. I wasn't expecting you. You don't have to do this, you know."

Having seen the state of her ranch, he had to disagree. "I think I do."

"There's no need to feel obligated. I'm sure you're up to your ears caring for your twins." She absently brushed hay strands from her jeans. "How are they, by the way?"

"Active," he answered. "Noisy. Up at all hours. Adorable. Perfect. And you were right about Mom—she's gone nuts over them. This is the happiest I've seen her since before Dad got sick."

"I'm glad," she replied, sincerity beaming

out of her warm smile. "So why are you here, instead of home with them?"

"I owe you." Did she think he was the kind of man to renege on his debts?

Her gaze widened on him and Jax swallowed hard, struck by the sparkle gleaming in her hazel eyes. They were a beautiful, swirling mixture of green and gold that he found quite captivating.

"Oh, that." She waved him away with a sweep of her hand. "I hereby absolve you of all your obligations inherent in offering yourself up for auction. Go live your life. Enjoy your babies. Be free."

She wasn't making this easy.

Go live his life? What life?

Until Faith and the twins had suddenly entered his life two days ago, he hadn't even realized that he hadn't been living—just going through the motions. He couldn't do that anymore.

He didn't want to.

He *owed* her, and not just because she had bought him at that silly auction.

Besides, she needed him, whether she was willing to admit it or not. And probably far more than she realized, if the state of her property was anything to go by.

"What are you doing?" he asked, ignoring the absolution of his commitment.

"Moving hay bales around. The guy who delivered them this morning dumped them right in the middle of my driveway and took off without a word. I've been hauling them one by one to the side of the barn. Hay bales are heavier than they look, by the way."

Jax chuckled. Toting hay bales wasn't much of a challenge for him. He could tote them two at a time and not even break a sweat, but then he was twice her size and had been doing it all of his life.

And why was she worrying about hay, anyway? Horses were a long time off, weren't they? First things first. Her house was falling down around her, and she was out here performing unnecessary manual labor?

"You could have called me."

She shook her head. "No. I can do this myself."

He lifted a brow. She was nothing if not stubborn. But he couldn't fault her for that. It took a tough person to handle life on a ranch. He wasn't convinced she was that person, but she certainly showed gumption.

"Can you give me a hand with the tarp?" She pressed one side of an olivegreen tarp into his hands, and he helped her unfold it.

Together they parachuted it over the top of the stack of hay.

"What are you pegging it down with?" he asked, scanning the ground for tent pegs and a mallet.

"Pegs?" Her brows lowered, crinkling over her nose. "Right. To keep the tarp from blowing away. I should have thought of that. I—" She stalled, dropping her gaze. "I don't know what I'll be using."

Of course she didn't. Now why wasn't Jax surprised? If ever he'd known someone completely unprepared for the challenges facing her, it was Faith Dugan. Initiative and good intentions could take a person only so far.

"I found the old tarp in a corner of the barn," she explained. "Maybe there are some pegs there, as well."

"Hold on a sec. I'll go look." Jax jogged into the barn, figuring he'd have a better chance of finding something that would work for the tarp, especially if they had to improvise.

He couldn't find any tent pegs, but he did locate some large nails that were long enough and thick enough to do the task. He grabbed a handful of them, along with a rusty old hammer that was hanging on the tool wall.

When he returned to Faith, she was standing with her back against the wall of hay, a distant gleam in her gaze. She looked tired, and for the first time he noticed the dark circles under her eyes.

She brightened when she saw what Jax was carrying.

"I know I must seem woefully ill-equipped to you," she admitted as Jax went to work nailing down the tarp. "It's a slow process, but I've been making a list of everything I'll be needing to keep the ranch running. I'll add pegs to the list, and maybe even an extra tarp or two."

That must be some list.

Jax fought against the smile that crept up the right side of his lips.

"So if you see anything you think I ought to add," she continued, obviously not seeing Jax's expression, "please speak up."

If it were anyone but Faith, he *would* have spoken. He would have told her how crazy her whole scheme was and how she should turn around and go back to wherever home was. He would have told her flat out how he doubted her ability to turn the falling-down-around-her house and equally scrappy outbuildings and land into a working ranch. Unless she was independently wealthy, she'd have money issues to add to what must already be multiple quandaries. Running a rescue operation on her own would be a challenge even on a tip-top ranch. Setting up her sanctuary while keeping the place from falling apart was a heavier load than any one person should be able to manage.

But Faith?

She was so—*so* earnest. She was obviously trying hard to make it work, and she wasn't about to take no for an answer. He didn't think she'd listen to him even if he did list all the reasons her plans would not work. She appeared dauntless, despite the mountains she was looking to scale. She didn't see the process as much as the end product.

Her dreams were real to her.

Vibrant.

And completely outrageous.

In some ways he envied her that outlook. He saw things in black-and-white. Mostly black. Definitely no pink—at least until his daughters had shown up in his life.

Either Faith didn't see the problems she was facing or she was making a conscious choice to ignore them. Of course, a rainbows-and-unicorns attitude would take her only so far. Eventually, she'd figure out that her operation was far too grand a scale for one woman. But he decided he wasn't going to be the one to bust her bubble. Not today.

"My first two horses are arriving right away," she informed him brightly as she tugged one of the ends of the tarp so he could nail it down.

Jax's hand slipped, and he slammed the hammer into his thumb. He yelped in pain and shook his hand in the air, then stuck it in his mouth to nurse it.

In an instant, Faith was crouched by his side, pulling her hand into hers. She examined him closely and murmured sweet nothings.

Jax was muttering, too. Something else.

"I'm fine," he insisted, snatching his hand out of her grip. His thumb was throbbing, and all he could think about was how soft and supple her palms and fingers were and how it was a shame ranch work would ruin them. Something was really messed up about that.

"At least let me get a bandage for you."

He uttered a sound that was half a laugh, half a scoff. "I don't need a bandage, Faith. Nothing's broken. The hammer didn't even pierce the skin."

Her expression fell, and only then did he realize she was offering a bandage because she wanted to do something for him. Because she felt sorry for him.

He hated it when that happened. Pity was the worst, even if it was over something as stupid as him being careless with a hammer and slamming it on his lousy thumb. He barely restrained himself from growling in frustration.

"I'm *fine*," he said again and then figured he'd better distract her before she ended up threatening to put his whole arm in a sling. "What's next after the hay?"

If she said *horses*, he was going to burst something.

"First things first. I need to fill the troughs with water from the pump."

He gaped at her but she didn't notice.

Did she realize how many trips it would take to fill a large trough with buckets of water from the pump? And that was to say nothing about the strain of doing all that pumping or hauling heavy buckets of water.

He sighed. This was going to be a long afternoon.

But apparently she was just getting warmed up.

"I figure I'll put hay down and hang an oat mixture in a bucket in the corral and then leave the gate to the front pasture open for easy access. I know the horses will need plenty of room to run, especially since they'll have been cooped up in a trailer for so long by the time they arrive here."

She pointed to the gate that led to a small meadow. Her plan would work in theory, if it wasn't for the terrible condition of the fences. The fence next to the road was in the worst shape. Wooden beams had been knocked about and some of the poles were completely unearthed.

Repairing that part alone would be a lot of work, but she could take her time with that—if she'd given herself time. The land wasn't going anywhere and neither were the fences. The problem was, there wasn't any time and there were a lot of fences. If the ones closest to the house were in this bad of condition, he dreaded to see what the rest of the thousand acres looked like.

Faith was a smart woman—she'd just never had to work on a ranch in such poor condition before. She still didn't understand just how much effort it would take to fix up this dump. She'd no doubt soon realize that his help alone would be nowhere near enough, even if he continued to help her, and at this point, he couldn't see how he could *not*. It wasn't in him to walk away from a lady in distress, even if the woman in question had bitten off far more than she could ever chew.

She'd said that she didn't have the money to hire any help, but he'd say she needed two wranglers at least. Worse, even if she had the funds, she might discover it was difficult to find a wrangler willing to work a horse farm—especially a sanctuary with wild horses. Serendipity was cattle country. Jax was one of the few who raised horses, and he trained his herd for cattle ranching.

Unlike many areas, the ranchers around Serendipity didn't necessarily object to horse farms. They just knew cattle. A wild-horse refuge? Some would believe it was a sad waste of good grazing land. There might be some resentment, although Jax hoped her neighbors would be better people than that.

Maybe she could find a teenager willing to do some work for her after school and on weekends. A youth working part-time wouldn't charge as much as a full-time professional wrangler. He had a couple of girls in mind who were especially good with horses. Before he brought his idea up to Faith, he decided he'd speak to the girls and their families to see if they were interested.

It would have to be soon, if Faith had horses coming in immediately.

"You're planning to fix the house up before you get too busy bringing in too many horses, right?"

He hadn't even seen the inside of the place, but based on everything else he'd viewed so far, he imagined it would be far from livable. "Are you staying at the Howells' Bed-and-Breakfast until you're ready to move in?"

It was a reasonable guess, seeing as there was no hotel in Serendipity. The Howells' B and B was the one and only place for guests in town to stay.

"Oh, I'm already moved into the house." She waved a hand as if to dismiss the thought. "I brought everything I needed to live on in my SUV."

He'd been thinking about the condition of the house itself, but moving her belongings was yet another hurdle to jump. She couldn't possibly have fit everything she owned into her SUV, even if it was one of the bigger models. What about her furniture? Dishes? Sheets and towels?

A toothbrush?

There might be a functional appliance or two inside the house, but Jax doubted Faith had found much in working condition. He imagined it would take weeks to put together anything remotely livable.

If she hadn't hired a moving company yet, he'd probably have to help her with that, as well. There was no way she would be able to move big furniture on her own, and even if she could, he wouldn't let her. He supposed he could always get his brothers to help with that. Their thick muscles were good for something, even if their thick heads were not.

"So you have the rest of your stuff left in storage somewhere?"

"Oh, no. I sold or gave away everything I wasn't bringing with me. I've got everything I need. I towed a horse trailer in with me. It's old and not pretty to look at, but it's reliable."

That was better. Not ideal, but better. He wouldn't have thought of moving his belongings in a horse trailer, but whatever worked for her. "I see. So you brought your furniture in your horse trailer, then. How bad is the interior of the house?"

She gazed at him as if he'd just grown a horn in the middle of his forehead. It wasn't as if he'd asked her to explain the theory of relativity—just how she planned to live in a house that raccoons and field mice probably rejected.

"Of course not. Why would I bring furniture in a horse trailer? That was for all my horsey stuff."

Horsey stuff?

It was all Jax could do not to burst out laughing, or smack his palm against his forehead or both. This woman had clearly tied her good sense to the top of her SUV on her way down to Texas and it had come loose from its binding and bounced off to the side of the road. On second thought, since no sane person would have bought this run-down ranch in the first place, maybe her good sense was something she'd lost a long time ago.

And didn't it just figure that *he'd* be the one to get caught up in this totally implausible and thoroughly ridiculous project?

As if he didn't have enough *totally implausible* drama brewing in his own house.

Had he stepped into some nutty alternate universe where everyday life was upside down and backward?

She hadn't really answered his question about the condition of the interior of her house. He was afraid to ask again, but he did it anyway.

"So you're—what? Camping out in your living room?"

Her smile was so fast and genuine that he found himself almost completely drawn into it.

"Pretty much. The Dennys left some furniture. It's not anywhere close to new condition, but I don't need much. I brought my sleeping bag, and the old couch is comfortable enough for now. There's no air conditioner, so it gets pretty hot in the daytime, but I'm outside most of the time anyway, so that won't matter. I open windows at night. I have plenty of food in the pantry. God is good. I have no complaints."

Maybe *she* didn't, but he did.

"Nevertheless, don't you think we ought to start by repairing the house?" It wasn't a suggestion, it was a rhetorical question, but Faith apparently interpreted it as if he were asking.

"Oh, my. No," she exclaimed, waving her hands in a dismissive motion. "I don't have time to worry about myself. My living conditions are just fine. I need your help to fix the front pasture." Her teeth nipped out and grabbed her bottom lip again as she thoughtfully surveyed the meadow in question. "I think we can lodge the horses in that field until I have enough time and resources to repair the other fences. I know the hay field is a disaster and I'll need to rotate the herd so they can graze, but one step at a time, right?"

Horses? Herd?

Jax felt as if he was tripping over those *steps* she mentioned.

"I can help mend fences," he offered cautiously. "But you're right. The perimeter is going to take a while to fully secure, not to mention the fences between pastures. The Dennys didn't happen to leave you a swather for the hay field, did they? It's severely overgrown. You should take care of that soon— you know, in all that free time you'll have because this place will be so easy to fix up."

He was teasing.

Kind of.

Her gaze widened in alarm, but when he curved his mouth up, she chuckled. "I thought you meant it needed to happen right now. Today."

"I'm sure we can borrow a swather from one of your neighbors when the time comes. Not today."

She nodded. "And the fence? How fast do you think you can help me fix the loose beams in the front meadow? I know I'm asking a lot out of you, but is there any possible way you can take care of it today?"

"Today?" he repeated, his voice tightening. He'd come over to see how she was settling in. She hadn't even been expecting him. And now she thought he was somehow going to be able to mend her impossibly unfixable property in a single afternoon? Did she realize

how labor intensive fence-mending was? And what would she have done if he hadn't shown up? Tried to handle it all herself? "Faith, you can't just—"

"But it's important," she interrupted. Red splashed across her cheeks. "You see, I've got a mare and her foal coming in this afternoon."

"This afternoon?" he roared, caught completely by surprise. When she'd said she was expecting horses to arrive right away, he thought she meant this month, or this week.

Not *today.*

Her eyes widened epically, and he realized he'd hurt her feelings, maybe even scared her. He took a mental step backward, lifted his hat by the crown and ran a hand through his hair.

"Look," he said, carefully modulating both the tenor and the tone of his voice. "I understand how important this is to you."

"Do you?" She folded her arms in a defensive gesture and narrowed her gaze on him. "Do you really? Because honestly, that's not what I'm getting from you."

He frowned and settled his hat back on his head. "Is that right?"

"Yes. I'm getting more of a grizzly-with-a-thorn-stuck-in-his-paw vibe. So if that's all you have to offer, then thank you, but I'd rather figure this out on my own." She was looking toward him but yet not really looking *at* him, her gaze just slightly averted.

Jax cringed. For a moment he'd thought Faith might be different. That she might be able to look beyond his scarred face to the man within. There had been a few minutes at the picnic when he'd thought they'd shared something, if not special, then at least normal.

But at the end of the day, she called it as she saw it—saw *him*.

A grizzly.

"If that's what you want," he muttered.

Even as he said the words, he knew he couldn't just walk away from Faith and leave her to do it all on her own. At the very least, there were plenty of fences to be mended, over many acres of land. He could do the work somewhere far away from the house and she wouldn't even have to know he'd been there.

If she didn't want him on her property, he wouldn't be able to fix up her house for her, at least not directly. But he would find others who could, people he trusted to do their best work and give her a good deal for it.

"Go." She choked out the word and pointed at his truck. "Just go."

"Yeah. Okay." He nodded and tipped his hat, conceding as graciously as he knew how.

His gut tightened painfully but he ignored it. "Best wishes to you with your hobby horses."

Hobby horses.
Hobby horses? Had he just referred to her future mustang rescue as a *hobby*?
"Jax."
He was halfway to his truck and didn't even bother to acknowledge her.
"Jax," she said again, her tone urgent as she hurried to catch up with him.
How rude of him to outright ignore her. Hadn't his mother taught him manners? She grabbed his elbow and yanked him around to face her.
"How dare you make fun of my work!"
He blew out a breath, ran a hand across his jaw and then lifted his hat and threaded his fingers through his thick dark brown curls.
"Look. That probably came out all wrong."
"Ya think?"
He held up a hand in surrender. "I didn't mean to insult you."
"Well, you—you—" she stammered. Tears welled in her eyes, and she dashed them away with the back of her hand.
Why, oh why did she have to cry when she got angry? The wetness gleaming in her eyes probably just reinforced everything Jax

was already thinking about her—that she was a fragile, foolish woman who bawled at the drop of a hat and couldn't possibly be successful running any kind of ranch, much less a wild-horse refuge.

When she finally dared to glance up at him, she didn't find judgment or censure in the chocolate depths of his eyes.

He looked as uncomfortable as all get-out and downright flustered.

Now, what did he have to be anxious about? She was the one who'd apparently planned herself into a corner—or rather, failed to plan enough for these early stages when there was so much that needed to be done.

Whatever it was, Jax wasn't taking her seriously. And that was a problem.

Fences or no fences, those horses would arrive in the space of a couple of hours, and she needed to be as prepared as possible for them. She'd thought she'd be further along. She was willing to admit it was taking her longer to perform what she'd expected to be simple ranch chores—chores she'd performed hundreds of times when she'd worked on ranches before. She hadn't allowed for the extra time it would take when she was working with run-down or missing equipment and no extra sets of hands. If she'd made mistakes—and she privately admitted she had—she would work it out.

She had to.

What she *didn't* have time for was to deal with this giant of a cowboy making fun of her and her work.

"Don't cry," he murmured, reaching out for her and then awkwardly dropping his arms again. "Please. I really didn't mean to—"

"I'm not crying," she snapped, dashing the wetness from her cheeks.

Stupid tears.

A muscle in the corner of his jaw ticked as his gaze followed the path of her hand. Clearly, he wasn't convinced. And why should he be?

He didn't believe anything about her—not that she was happy living simply for the time being while she funneled all her time and resources into her horses, or even that she was capable of running this rescue at all.

Maybe he was right.

The niggling doubt that haunted her late at night when she couldn't sleep worked its way into her chest, pressing into her lungs and making it difficult for her to breathe. Adrenaline coursed through her, the fight-or-flight instinct that challenged her to run away from the difficult and unknown.

She chose Door #1. She would fight. She would not run. She would do this thing, and no cowboy—or a whole herd of them—was going to convince her otherwise.

She was just barely managing to tamp her hidden anxieties back into the recesses of her mind when a shiny new red truck pulled into her driveway, hauling an incongruently beat-up two-horse trailer.

Oh, no.

Panic revved Faith's pulse even more, charging it into overdrive, and heat flushed her face.

They were here. Her first rescue horses were here.

She had Alban, her riding horse, already stabled. These were her mustangs. Wild and untamed and Faith planned to let them stay that way.

Marta Stevens from the Mustang Mission in Wyoming waved out the window and then pulled her truck around, slowly backing the trailer toward the side corral gate.

Faith had thought she would have a bigger window of time before Marta arrived. Two hours wouldn't have been enough, of course, as Jax had so handily pointed out. But—

"Your horses, I presume?"

Faith expected Jax's voice to be laced with

sarcasm, but surprisingly, it wasn't. Not too much, anyway. Mostly, he sounded only vaguely amused and very tired.

Of course he was tired. What was he even doing here with her? She felt suddenly guilty that she was asking him to spend his day mending fences for her. Why he was helping her out when he'd no doubt spent the weekend getting to know his twins was beyond her comprehension. He must be exhausted beyond belief, and yet here he was.

With her. And her horses.

"You ready?" he asked, leaning an elbow against the corral fence.

All she could do was nod. Words escaped her. There was no way to describe what she was feeling right now. She was so excited she thought her heart might burst. She'd dreamed of this day for so long that it hardly felt real. Her whole life culminated in this moment.

Past, present and future converged.

Her feet were frozen to the spot, and she was unable even to breathe. She should probably be doing—something. She wasn't sure what.

Jax watched her, his gaze unreadable. "Give me a second, will you?"

He stepped to the side and fished his cell

phone out of its holder. She assumed he was checking on his twins.

She shifted her attention to the trailer, and she surveyed the corral with a critical eye. There were a couple of loose beams, but it wasn't as bad as it might have been. If a horse wanted to get out, it would. No question. But there was at least the hint of containment. Faith prayed that would be enough.

"How are they?" she asked as Jax returned to her side.

"What? Who?"

She raised her eyebrows. "Why, Rose and Violet, of course. Who did you think I was talking about?"

He chuckled. "Oh, yeah. Right. My mom is having the time of her life with them. They're doing great. But she's not the only one I called. My brothers, Slade and Nick, are on their way over to work on your fences for you."

"They are?" Her throat tightened with emotion. Jax didn't have to be here today, and he could have driven off without a word. After all, she'd ordered him to do so.

Instead, he was calling in reinforcements. She'd never be able to aptly express her gratitude, much less repay him for his kindness.

"I'll take care of the fences around the front

pasture," he said. "Between the three of us we ought to be able to get it in working order within a couple of hours. Not perfect, mind you, but serviceable for the moment."

Faith sent up a silent prayer of appreciation.

"But the horses are already here. I'm sure they aren't comfortable in the trailer." If she could hear the discouragement in her tone, she was positive he did. After all, she was pretty much admitting she was everything he thought she was.

Flighty. Foolish. Unprepared.

"Yes, the horses are here," was all he said. He shoved his hands into the front pockets of his jeans and rocked back on his heels. He glanced down at her expectantly.

As if she knew what to do and he was just waiting for her to do—whatever. But she *didn't* know what to do.

Was he *smiling*?

She couldn't quite be positive because of the scar, but still. His expression was both annoying and unfair.

Annoying, because he knew more than she ever would about raising horses and he knew it, and unfair because—because of the butter-flies his hint of a grin sent whirling through her stomach, made more intriguing by the mystery inherent in his smile.

"Marta must have made exceptionally good time. She wasn't supposed to be here for a couple of hours yet," she said with a defensive tilt of her chin.

"And yet, here they are."

She narrowed her gaze on him and he chuckled.

Marta hopped out of the red truck's cab and rushed toward Faith, laughing and enveloping her in an animated hug, nearly knocking both of them off their feet in her enthusiasm.

"Your first horses," Marta exclaimed, continuing to hug the stuffing out of Faith. "Trust me, you'll remember this day for the rest of your life."

"I'll say," Jax said under his breath, a low rumble emerging from his chest.

Faith rolled her eyes at him. "Marta, this is Jax. Jax, this is Marta from Mustang Mission in Wyoming."

Jax extended his hand, but Marta was slow to respond, staring at Jax's scar. Jax uncompromisingly met her gaze, and she winced and quickly averted her eyes.

His shoulders tightened and his brown eyes flashed with anguish as he dropped his arm to his side. Faith glimpsed one second of the depth of the pain he was experiencing and then it was gone, hardening along with the line of his lips. Clearly this wasn't the first time someone had been taken aback by his injury.

Personally, Faith didn't get it. The scars showed that he was strong—a survivor. How was that a bad thing? And anyway, a man was made by his heart, not his face, and from what she knew of Jax, he was pure gold. She'd never been the type of person who averted her gaze from someone with an injury or disability. Jax might look like a bear of a man, but he had feelings, too, even if he kept them well under wraps.

"I can't wait for you to meet my horses," Faith said a little too brightly, desperate to distract him. "The mama is Willow and her colt is Pilgrim."

Jax turned his attention to Faith, allowing her to drag him to the rear of the trailer. He unlatched the hook and carefully opened the doors to reveal a bay-and-white pinto mare and her nearly identical offspring.

The skittish colt bucked his back legs and tossed his head. When he turned to look at her, Faith was startled to find he had one brown eye and one blue. How beautiful and rare he was. Her heart leaped into her throat, overflowing with the joy of discovery. Her first horses, and she'd managed to score a gorgeous, unique mustang beyond what she could ever have imagined. How blessed she was.

Her joy quickly muted when she caught sight of the mare's stark condition. Her entire rib cage was as visible as a xylophone, and her flanks poked nearly out of the skin. The poor thing had very little flesh on her bones at all. Her coat was dull and patches of hair were falling out. It was a wonder she'd birthed a healthy foal at all in the shape she was in.

"Do you see?" she whispered, laying a hand on Jax's elbow. "Do you understand now?"

He looked down at her and nodded. "I see why you're rushing things. Do you mind?" He gestured toward the mare.

"Please."

Jax spoke to the horse in a low, rich, lyrical tone. The mare pricked up her ears. Faith thought she might spook as the colt had done, but she just shivered.

"Easy there, girl." Jax's voice held such a calming effect that even Faith felt soothed by the gentle vocal caress. "You don't want to upset your little one. It's all good. We're going to take care of you. No worries. You're home now."

Home.

Faith's chest was full to bursting. These horses were home, and they would benefit from every bit of her time and attention. With her help, Willow would regain the weight she'd lost and her coat would turn shiny and beautiful again. Her colt would grow up happy and free.

Free to live.

Free to run on Faith's thousand acres.

Free to flourish as wild horses should, with no man-made expectations or agenda.

It was only a few more minutes before Jax's brothers arrived. Slade perused the front meadow and made the same estimate Jax had—one or two hours of labor at the most. Tools in hand, he and Nick headed out to the fence line.

"I think we can unload the horses into the corral now," Jax said, unhooking the rope strung across the back of the trailer. "I'm sure they want to stretch their legs."

Faith agreed, but she was bumping up against her fear and her inexperience. Back in Wyoming, where she'd worked as a volunteer, she'd rarely dealt with the newly arrived horses—settling them in was left to the more experienced staff, who would be better prepared to deal with any problems. On top of that, Marta's trailer was an older model.

It didn't have a side door to disembark the horses. It didn't even have a ramp in the back. She'd somehow have to convince the horses to back out of the trailer, and she wasn't even sure if they would take a halter.

There were so many things she didn't know. Embarrassment coursed through her. She cast her gaze downward, afraid Marta, or worse, Jax, would see the panic in her eyes. Her pulse was pounding so hard she thought they might be able to hear it.

She needed help but she didn't know how to ask for it.

How *did* one unload a wild mustang from an old trailer?

She glanced up and found Jax staring right at her, his gaze narrowed as if he was trying to figure her out.

Fat chance of that.

She was an enigma even to herself at times, now being one of them. She was at once as excited and as scared as she'd ever been in her life. She couldn't imagine the plethora of expressions that must be flittering across her face. It was no wonder Jax was staring.

Jax's eyes glittered as he opened the corral gate adjacent to the rear of the trailer, effectively creating one side of a chute.

Marta moved to the other side and widened her arms to block off that path as best she could. Jax briefly caught Faith's gaze and tipped his head, encouraging her to do the same.

Faith held her breath as Jax strode up to the trailer, his voice and his steps slow, even and confident. She marveled at his rich, melodious tone. She didn't think she would ever get tired of hearing Jax speak, at least to the horses.

The mare tensed when he laid a gentle hand on her flank, but she didn't buck or try to bolt. Jax took his time, talking, talking and talking some more as he slid his palm up her back and onto her neck.

He stopped for a moment and allowed her to get used to his presence and his scent. He wasn't in a hurry. He appeared perfectly at ease, intently attuned to the animal, communicating with words and without. It was a wondrous sight to behold, and it took Faith's breath away.

When Jo had said Jax was a genius with horses, she hadn't been kidding. Faith had never seen anything like it.

After another minute had passed, Jax slipped his arm under Willow's neck and pressed gently, urging the horse to step backward. Every time she balked or protested, every time her nostrils flared or her ears pinned back, Jax would stop and wait until she was once again calm and in tune with his own serenity. He displayed endless patience, coaxing Willow backward and chuckling when the foal nudged his thigh with his muzzle, impatient for it to be his turn for attention.

He backed the mare up until her rear legs were on solid ground. Willow shifted and tossed her head but Jax took it in stride, his melodic murmuring never ceasing.

"One more step, girl. You can do it. I know you can. And then you and your little one will be free to run."

If Faith didn't know better, she would have thought that the mare understood Jax's words, for in a moment more he had her off the trailer and into the corral with her colt right on her heels.

"Success," Marta cheered, closing the gate behind Faith, who had followed the horses in. "You've got a good one there, Faith."

"I know." She smiled at her friend and mentor. "I appreciate you bringing her out to me. I promise I'll take good care of her."

Marta laughed and nodded toward Jax, who was still by Willow's side, running his hands down her neck and head. "I meant *him*."

Heat rose to Faith's cheeks. "Oh."

Marta's chuckle turned into a full-blown laugh. She was right, though. Jax's way with horses was nothing short of extraordinary. She'd never seen anything like it. The Lord had truly guided her hand—or rather, her pocketbook—when she'd bid on Jax at the auction.

But she certainly didn't want Marta to get the wrong impression.

"Jax?" Faith tried to sound surprised. She waved offhandedly. "He—he's just helping me out today. Those are his brothers out there mending the fences."

Marta's green eyes gleamed at her. "Is he married?"

"What? No." And with what had just happened to the poor man on the home front, Faith doubted he'd be remotely interested in *that* particular institution in the near future.

Or ever again.

And neither, for that matter, was she.

But Marta already knew Faith's story, and Faith had no business discussing Jax's, so instead she just smiled and let Marta think whatever she wanted to.

"You've just brought me the true loves of my life," she reminded her friend. "Willow and Pilgrim. I'm sure they're going to keep me plenty busy."

And Jax?

She didn't know what he was. Helpful, maybe. Useful, sometimes.

But mostly, he was a complication she simply didn't need in her life. And she'd keep telling herself that until she believed it.

Chapter Four

Jax yanked the last corner of a yellow fitted crib sheet over the mattress until it finally slipped into place. He grunted with satisfaction.

One crib down, one to go, and finally the twins would be able to graduate from the bassinet and into the cribs in their nursery. In the three weeks since they'd been dropped on his doorstep, Rose and Violet had flourished. They were already growing like nobody's business, and Jax couldn't be prouder.

From her view in a nearby bouncy chair, Rose babbled at him as if providing him with instructions, her chunky arms pumping in delight. Violet, whom Jax had quickly recognized as the quieter of the two twins, sucked on her tiny fist and stared at him with her wise brown eyes.

It was hard to believe that he ever had had trouble telling these two beautiful babies apart. Now he recognized both on sight and could tell one from the other as much by personality as by looks.

"You think so, huh?" he asked, addressing Rose. He chuckled. Look at him, talking to a newborn baby as if she could understand his words. As if he understood her replies.

In the most peculiar way, he kind of did. In the three weeks he'd had the children, he'd learned how to interpret their sounds and cries. He could differentiate between whether they were wet, needed a bottle or if their little tummies were hurting them.

Sometimes it was none of the above. Sometimes they were scared or lonely and just wanted to be held, and he was okay with that. He liked snuggle time. One cowboy and two babies didn't seem like much of a fair match, but he thought he was managing surprisingly well, all things considered, and even more surprising, enjoying every minute of it.

This was uncharted territory, after all.

Most folks had nine months to prepare for a newborn. He hadn't had a single second, which explained why he was just now completing the transition of his spare room into a nursery. His mother had decorated the place with pink frilly curtains and pink and white kittens on the wall. He drew the line at pink crib sheets and had chosen a more neutral yellow color.

A man could take only so much pink, after all.

Like Jax, Faith was treading new ground. He often thought about her out there all by herself with her horses. He still meant to find her a couple of teenage wranglers. It had been on his to-do list since day one, but he simply hadn't found time, what with taking care of the twins and all.

He'd been over to Faith's place a few times over the past weeks, not so much out of obligation as curiosity. She had officially released him from his commitment to her, so that wasn't a factor, and yet he kept finding reasons to go visit her.

Untamed Mustang Refuge, she'd named the place. She planned to advertise the moniker with a large post sign at the front of the driveway, but paying for something like that would be a long time out yet. She did have funds—she'd explained to him about all the money she'd saved over the years, looking forward to this dream—but she was spending it only on things that directly benefited the horses. Stubborn woman still refused to put any time and effort into her own house or any part of her property that wasn't specifically mustang related.

She was all about her horses. He had to give her that.

"I hope you and your sister grow up to be as tough and resilient as Faith Dugan," he told Rose as he picked her up and offered her a bottle.

Every time he'd come by to visit her, she'd been out with the mustangs—mending fences, pitching hay and toting water from the well pump to the trough. Hard labor, especially for a woman who, for the past few years, had been able to do this kind of work only by volunteering a few hours a day on weekends. Nonstop physical work, day in and day out, was new to her. He'd noticed the blisters on her hands and the sunburn on her cheeks. But she never complained, and she never slowed down. Nothing put her off course. He wouldn't be surprised if she ate her own meals out in the meadow with her mustangs.

With his help, and the aid of Nick and Slade, who'd come out a few more times, she'd managed to mend most of the major fences around her property, although it would still be some time before she would be able to address every beam and pole on her thousand-acre spread. But she'd done enough to give the mustangs plenty of room to safely run.

Willow was already looking markedly better. Her ribs weren't showing as much, and her coat was quickly regaining its shine. Faith had mentioned something about adding to her herd soon—well, a mare and a foal hardly constituted a *herd*, but he knew what she meant.

His lips curved upward and he shook his head. He didn't know why thinking about Faith and her hobby horses made him smile. It just did.

She did.

His phone rang, and he fished it from its holster, expecting it to be his mom or one of his brothers checking up on him. They'd all been hovering over him the past few weeks to the point where he was beginning to wonder if they all thought he was completely inept at being a father.

He glanced down at the screen, and his gaze widened.

Faith?

Why was she calling him? He'd given her his number in case she wanted to consult him about any of her ranch projects, but she'd never reached out to him.

"Hey, Faith. What's up?" he asked, shifting Rose to the crook of his elbow and propping the bottle with his chin while he used his other hand to hold his phone to his ear. Violet fussed from her chair, so he bounced it with one foot. All he needed was a stick and a plate to balance on the other foot and he'd be a regular circus act.

"Jax!"

The panic in Faith's voice brought him to instant alertness. Electricity popped through him. He must have jerked his head, because the bottle slipped from under his chin, hit the floor by his boots and rolled underneath the crib.

He grumbled something unintelligible.

"What's the matter?" He stooped and reached for the bottle. Rose screeched her discontent. Even Violet jumped into the fray, and he went from feeling as if he finally had it together with the twins to a total loss of control in half a second.

And then there was the woman on the other end of the line. Faith sniffled and swept in a shaky, audible breath. Jax's protective instinct sparked to life and swirled through his chest, lodging in his throat.

"What's wrong?" he asked again when she didn't immediately answer.

"I'm s-sorry. I can hear that you have your hands full with your babies. I just— I didn't know who else to call."

"Faith." He stated her name firmly and calmly. She had to get her emotions under control, or he would never be able to figure out what was going on with her. "Tell me what has you so flustered."

"I called the vet but he's out of town."

"A problem with one of the horses, then?"

"Yes, I—" She paused and hiccupped. "My new stallion. Fuego. I only just brought him and a couple of other horses up to the ranch over the weekend. I thought everything was going remarkably well. The herd accepted him immediately as their leader and he acknowledged them as his band. But then today—well, I'm trying to build a shelter in the front meadow so the horses have plenty of shade. There's lumber everywhere. I didn't even think about…"

Again she paused. He lowered his brows. She wasn't making any sense.

"The herd usually keeps its distance, especially when I'm working on a project. I'm not very good with a hammer and I make an awful racket. So it didn't even occur to me to worry about closing the gate to the front meadow. And then Fuego—I don't know why, I didn't provoke him, but he charged me. Straight through the pile of lumber."

"Are you hurt?" he demanded, already buckling a still-crying Rose into her car seat and tucking her bottle into the nearby diaper bag.

Adrenaline pounded through him at the thought of Faith being injured. Wild stallions were nothing to mess around with, and Faith had no one out there to keep her safe. She loved those silly horses so much, he knew she'd put herself into the path of danger before she risked hurting one of the mustangs.

Just how bad had it gotten this time? He clung to the thought that she was well enough to call him—and that she was allowing herself to ask for help. It was a start.

He only hoped she wasn't too late in asking.

"Me? No. No. I'm fine. Don't worry about me." She sounded confused that he'd even asked the question. "The thing is, Fuego never made it to me. His hooves got tangled up in some lumber, and he fell onto his back. He's not getting up, Jax. What if he— Oh, Jax, I—"

Jax's jaw tightened with strain. He hoped the stallion wasn't as bad off as all that, but if the injury was as serious as it sounded, this was going to be an especially rough day for Faith, who wasn't ready for the harsher realities of ranch life. Putting down an injured animal was a difficult but sometimes necessary part of living in the country.

Sometimes the best thing for the animal was the hardest for the human being involved.

Especially a woman with a heart as sweet and tender as Faith's.

He clenched his jaw. He hated to be the one who might have to introduce her to the severe side of the life she'd chosen for herself, but it couldn't be helped.

She needed him. Now more than ever.

"I'll be right over."

"Thank you."

"And Faith?"

"Yes?"

"Please don't do anything until I get there. Do you understand? Stay right where you are and don't move." Pictures of Faith being taken down by a terrified, injured stallion flashed across his mind.

"Yes, Jax. I will. Just please. Hurry."

She didn't have to tell him twice. He couldn't get to Faith's ranch fast enough. His mother was out shopping in San Antonio, and there was no time to call in his brothers, so he was on his own with the twins. He strapped Violet into her car seat, then jogged around the house frantically grabbing whatever baby items he thought might be necessary and jamming them in the diaper bag. He slipped the strap over his head and onto one shoulder and grabbed both car seats, one in each hand.

It took him longer than he would have liked to figure out how the car seats snapped into the base. He really should have paid more attention when his mother was showing him how it was done, but until now she'd always been there to help him.

Once on the road, he forced himself to drive the speed limit for the twins' sake, but his heart was thumping heavily in his chest like the beat of a clock. The stallion's condition might be worsening with every second that went by—and that was to say nothing about Faith's safety.

She'd promised him she'd wait for him to get there, but he knew it couldn't be easy for her, standing around and doing nothing while one of her beloved horses suffered.

He was afraid the worst part was yet to come.

Faith breathed a huge sigh of relief when Jax strode up, a car seat in each hand and a diaper bag slung over his shoulder. She'd never been happier to see someone in her entire life. To think he'd dropped everything and rushed over with two babies in tow. Gratitude welled in her chest, mixing with the anxiety already lurking there.

She felt horribly guilty that she'd had to interrupt his day with his children, but she hadn't been joking when she'd said she knew of no one else to call. It was the first time she'd truly felt alone on her ranch.

And worse than that—*helpless.*

She'd almost had a heart attack when Fuego had gone down, and the sound he made— She hoped she'd never have to hear anything like that ever again.

He'd rolled from side to side a couple of times, snorting and flailing his legs, but in the end he hadn't stood up. He'd shaken and shivered and whinnied in distress but had not regained his footing.

Faith feared for the worst.

What if Fuego's leg couldn't be mended, even with surgery? She'd have to put the beautiful silver stallion down, and it would break her heart. Nothing she'd ever experienced on a ranch could have prepared her for a situation like this.

Jax would know how to proceed. He would

be able to determine if the stallion could be saved. She trusted him to do what was best.

Big, strong, solid, dependable Jax.

He hesitated, glancing down at his daughters, fast asleep in their seats. "Can you watch these two sweethearts while I—" He gestured to the half-built shelter. "I'd rather keep them safely away from the drama, if you don't mind."

When she nodded, he placed the car seats in the shade next to the barn and strode toward Fuego, a frown creasing his brow. He stood silently for a few moments, his hands on his hips, evaluating the stallion.

She didn't know what she expected—for Jax to run straight for the horse and help the stallion regain his feet on sheer strength alone? Was that even possible?

Jax was a large man, but even he didn't have enough muscles to lift a thousand-pound animal, especially a frightened one that would be thrashing and aggressive. She thought maybe he might examine Fuego's legs with his hands to try to determine if there was any serious damage, but if he got that close, then he'd run the risk of getting kicked by those vicious hooves.

He didn't try to right the horse, nor did he check Fuego's legs for wounds. Instead, he slowly and steadily walked around the lumber pile, occasionally pushing a beam aside with his boot. He assessed the situation without approaching the wild-eyed animal. He spoke to the horse in the rich, lyrical tone Faith now thought of as his horse-whisperer voice, although she knew he would pitch a fit if she ever said such a thing out loud. But that was what it was. It reassured and calmed even the most frightened or spooked of horses.

Even with Jax there, Faith wasn't convinced all would be well with Fuego, but her heart responded peculiarly to the tenor of his voice. It had the same effect on her as it had on the horse. Calming. Hypnotic. Lulling her pulse to a gentler, steadier rhythm.

He crouched by the horse's head and stroked its neck. Fuego thrashed and made another terrifying, heart-rending squeal. Jax adjusted his position so he wouldn't get kicked but left his hand on the stallion's shoulder.

"Easy there, boy," he coaxed. "You've got yourself into a real pickle this time, haven't you? Serves you right for trying to charge a pretty woman. You should know better. Just be your handsome self and the women will come to you."

The horse slowly stilled under the sound of

Jax's voice. "Let's have a look at those legs, shall we?"

Violet made a mewling sound that caught Faith's attention. She guessed the baby had been woken by Fuego's disturbance. She unbuckled the infant's car seat and sheltered the infant in her arms.

The act of soothing the child had the additional benefit of calming her, as well.

"Your daddy came to the rescue," she informed little Violet in a whisper. "He'll be able to help Fuego. I know he will."

She stared down at the wide-eyed infant, and her heart welled with compassion for the little one. "I know your life hasn't always been ideal, but you've got your daddy now. He'll do right by you, you know. And you've got—" She stopped herself before she could say the words hovering on her lips. *You've got me.*

No.

These two little girls were coming to mean so much to her—too much. But she could not let herself get involved, not without risking her whole world imploding.

Hadn't she learned anything from last time?

With effort she willed her emotions back, folding them up and tucking them deep inside her heart. She would not come to care meaningfully for these children. She could not. They would be a neighbor's children and that was all. She had no place in their lives and they had no place in hers. And neither did their father.

She'd called upon Jax because he was an expert with horses and because he was still one of only a few townspeople she'd met so far. In an emergency—and this definitely qualified as one—she hadn't known whom else to call.

It had nothing to do with the spark of attraction that surfaced between them every time their eyes met. It wasn't because the reflection in his gaze suggested that the chemistry she felt might be reciprocated. It wasn't because of his tenderness or thoughtfulness, nor even that he'd offered his time and talents even when she'd assured him it wasn't necessary for him to do so.

And it had nothing to do with the way he'd dropped everything to come to her rescue.

What sent a jolt of dread skittering from nerve to nerve until her whole frame was quivering was the way she couldn't stop her chest from expanding when she gazed down at Jax's two precious infants.

She didn't dare make a connection, come to care for these tiny pieces of humanity. These soft, sweet, innocent twins.

She wiped a hand across her suddenly wet eyes.

No. She couldn't do this, couldn't become involved.

She had her reasons—good ones—and one of them was Jax himself, embroiled in a bizarre and complicated relationship with his ex-wife.

And then she had her own issues. She knew her limits. Caring too much was her Achilles' heel. It invariably got her in trouble.

She invested her heart in the wrong places— in the wrong *people*. It had taken an utter heartbreak for her to learn that hard truth, and it was the reason she had chosen to go it alone with her wild-horse rescue.

Except she wasn't going it alone.

Jax was here.

He'd turned his attention from the stallion to the piles of timber surrounding him, hemming him in. Still speaking in low murmurs, he moved beam after beam, tossing them to the side to give Fuego more room to move.

Why hadn't she thought to do that?

He'd nearly cleared a path for the stallion

when suddenly the horse neighed loudly and rolled, unaided and snorting, to his feet. He shook his mane and bucked twice.

Faith breathed a sigh of relief. Clearly Fuego's legs weren't broken. All was well.

And then, in the blink of an eye, the stallion put down his head and charged. Faith's adrenaline roared to life, and yet events seemed to unfold in slow motion.

"Jax!" she screamed.

Jax had his back to the horse. He didn't even see it coming. He dropped the beam he was holding and half turned toward her—and away from the horse. She'd unwittingly made his situation worse.

Fuego hit Jax with a momentum that would have sent most men sprawling in the dirt. It was almost as if Jax sensed the thousand-pound collision just moments before it happened. He ducked and dodged to the side.

The horse hit his left shoulder. Jax staggered and his hat hit the dirt, but he kept on his feet in the shuffle, running several steps to regain his balance.

Faith's heart was beating frantically in her ears.

Oh, Jax.

He could very easily have been trampled

under the powerful stallion's hooves, and all because she'd messed up. She was the one who had placed the lumber where the horses could potentially hurt themselves. Jax wouldn't be here if it wasn't for her.

Another epic failure in a long stream of them, it seemed, one of many in the weeks since she'd arrived in Serendipity. Compared with her much smaller list of accomplishments, she was feeling rather low and pathetic. And she needed to apologize to Jax once again.

It was becoming a habit she would rather break.

Jax stooped to retrieve his hat, and Faith realized that Rose had woken. Both babies were howling in protest, playing off each other to see who could cry the loudest. Her attention had been so rapt on the interplay between Jax and Fuego that she hadn't even heard the poor darlings.

It was no surprise that they were bawling. In pure terror, Faith had just screamed their father's name loud enough to wake the entire town, and these poor little babies were well within hearing distance.

No infant should have to wake up to that.

"It's okay, my sweethearts," she cooed. She

considered trying to remove Rose from her car seat, but she was already holding Violet, and it would be difficult to unlatch the buckle with one hand. Plus she'd have to juggle two babies at once, which she wasn't certain she could do.

She could only imagine Jax's learning curve with his twins. How did he manage caring for two babies at once?

For the first time since she'd arrived in Serendipity, she regretted that her house was a certified wreck. It wasn't fit for adult visitors, much less a couple of newborn babies. She couldn't invite them in and let the little ones down on the floor anytime soon.

Jax flashed a smile at Faith as he reached the barn and effortlessly scooped Rose into his arms. Rose immediately quieted, even before he spoke to her.

"It's okay, little darlin'," he murmured, brushing a soft kiss over her downy forehead. "Daddy's fine. Fuego is fine. Everything is okay now."

Faith breathed a silent prayer of gratitude.

Jax turned to plant a kiss on Violet's forehead, and Faith's gaze narrowed on the sleeve of his navy blue T-shirt. Fabric hung in tatters over the shoulder and a copper-red stain was spreading in uneven patterns across the surface.

Faith gasped and reached for his elbow to still him. "Jax! You're not fine. You're bleeding."

Chapter Five

Jax glanced at his left arm and shrugged. "Don't worry about it. It's nothing."

The expression on Faith's face was priceless—going from startled to confused to angry in a matter of seconds. Her face flushed from peach to cherry red. Her expressions were so distinct from each other that they reminded Jax of one of those old flip comic books that demonstrated basic animation.

When she gathered her brows over her eyes and her expression slammed to a halt on *determined* with a dash of *stubborn*, he knew he was in trouble.

He'd seen that look before, and it didn't bode well for him. He didn't see why she was making such a big deal out of the gash, anyway. It was just a little blood. He'd had worse.

Much worse.

"I'd better be going," he said, rather than allowing his mind to dwell upon the *worse*. "The babies need to be fed. I think Fuego is out of the woods now, but keep an eye on him and call the vet for a follow-up appointment just to be on the safe side. Watch for any signs of lameness."

"If the babies need to be fed, we'll feed them here, together, but there is no way I'm letting you drive off this property in that condition."

She seemed determined to bandage him up, and he couldn't restrain the shudder that went through him at the prospect. This wasn't about the gash or the blood or even the pain. This was about him leaving before she got a good look at his upper arm.

Her grip on his elbow tightened. "Come inside. My house is not pretty but it's functional. You can feed the twins while I gather some bandages and antibacterial ointment." She frowned. "I think I know where my first-aid kit is. I've had to use it often in the past few weeks on my own splinters and blisters."

She was rambling, more to herself than to him, and for some reason he found her little quirk amusing, like a mama bird chirping over her chicks. He just wished he wasn't the injured chick. She was about to see more than she bargained for.

"Sit down," she encouraged him, nodding toward a burnt-orange armchair that had clearly seen better days. It was probably older than Jax was, but he found it surprisingly comfortable when he sank back into the cushion and crossed his left ankle over his right knee. Having had much practice recently in the art and craft of child-propping, he deftly supported Rose within the triangle of his legs.

"Here we go, then," he told Rose, wishing he felt as confident as his tone. He was surprised his voice wasn't shaky. "Apparently your auntie Faith is going to patch up Daddy's owie."

One of them, at least.

His entire life had changed for the worse because of the accident, because of these ugly scars he carried on his body and in his heart. Some were visible to the eye. Others were known only by him. His family might suspect that the damage ran deeper than what he'd admitted aloud, but he tried to keep the bulk of his pain and shame to himself.

He didn't care to share either his inward or outward disfigurement with anyone. That Faith was about to discover a hidden wound somehow made it all that much worse. They were friends, he thought, and it was only recently that he'd realized he had far too few of those. It was his own fault. He'd alienated those who'd reached out to him after his accident. He didn't want to ruin his newfound friendship with Faith.

She wasn't a superficial woman. She seemed to be able to see beyond the puckered scar on his face and glimpse the man within. But maybe it was only that she was too wrapped up in her own problems to look—really *look*—at him.

And that was about to change.

He knew how irrational his emotions were. The physical scars were inconsequential. They shouldn't matter, but the pain of Susie's revulsion was still too fresh in his mind. He remembered in vivid detail the day—

"I found it," Faith said, sounding out of breath as she burst into the living room with Violet in one arm and a white tackle box–looking thing in the other. "This has a little bit of everything. I bought it at Emerson's Hardware the first day I was in town. I was stocking up on supplies and wasn't sure what I needed. That Eddie Emerson is such a sweet guy. He walked me through the store and made lots of suggestions."

Sweet guy.

Jax didn't know why he bristled at the words. He had no claim on Faith, nor did he want to.

Eddie was, in fact, a good guy, at least as far as Jax could discern. He worked hard at his family's store, he attended church every Sunday, and he was popular with the ladies. If Faith was interested in him, she could do worse.

Jax's gaze swept over Faith and abruptly changed his mind. Eddie was too young for her. He was still figuring out who he was. Faith had lived with the harsh realities of real life. She hadn't spoken of them, but he could see it in the way her eyes glazed over sometimes as memories overtook her and in the sad shadows that sometimes accompanied those moments.

Faith placed Violet in her car seat and then rummaged through the diaper bag and withdrew two empty bottles and a can of formula.

"That's the difference between a small town and a big city," she informed him.

He wondered if she realized she was carrying the whole conversation on her own. Jax was afraid anything he said right now would come out sounding bitter, so he remained silent.

"Back in Connecticut, where I was born and raised, shopping experiences are on the opposite side of the spectrum. Most often you can't find a store employee to help you even if you're looking for one, and if you do somehow manage to flag one down, they drag their feet and don't give any more assistance than absolutely necessary." She paused and gave this cute little feminine snort. "And don't even get me started on trying to find someone to help you carry out a large load of material. It would be better if we didn't even talk about the headaches you'll find there."

Okay.

He grinned. He wasn't *talking* about anything. She wouldn't let him get a word in edgewise.

She disappeared into what he assumed was the kitchen and reappeared moments later with two warm bottles of formula.

"I tested the temperature on the inside of my wrist. That's right, isn't it?"

He chuckled and nodded.

She already knew the answer to her question—she was just giving him the opportunity to show off his new daddy knowledge. "Okay, good. Anyway, back to Emerson's." She picked up the conversation right where she'd left off. Jax wondered how rude it would sound to tell her he didn't want to talk about Eddie Emerson anymore.

"I couldn't believe it when I walked in the door. Eddie came right around the counter with a welcoming smile on his face and didn't leave my side until he was satisfied I'd found everything I needed."

Jax had been born and raised in Serendipity and had worked the family ranch all his life. He visited San Antonio for supplies when he absolutely had to, but mostly he kept to himself and shopped in Serendipity.

He liked the country. He'd never once considered leaving the town, but he had to admit he'd never taken the time to see it through a newcomer's eyes. Faith was beaming, and in the oddest way, it made Jax proud to call Serendipity home.

"That looks terrible," Faith said, moving to his side to examine his bloody sleeve. "Do you think you can mind both babies while I tend to your injury?"

He chuckled. He'd learned to do a lot of things in pairs since his daughters had come into his life.

"Observe," he said mildly.

Faith set Violet into the curve of his right arm and he propped her bottle with his left hand, then gestured for Faith to hand him the other bottle in his right. Exhibiting yet another circus-worthy feat, he aimed carefully and managed to connect the tip of the bottle with Rose's smacking lips.

He grinned in triumph.

"I am duly impressed." Faith laughed and applauded. "Well done, Daddy."

She perched on the corner of the coffee table and rummaged through the first-aid kit, removing gauze, alcohol swabs, tape and antibacterial ointment.

"Let's see what we've got here," she said, reaching for the sleeve on his T-shirt.

A monster.

He strove to hold himself steady as she rolled up the sleeve, bit by excruciating bit, apologizing profusely when he sucked in a ragged breath. The stupid scar tissue was ultrasensitive, and despite what he'd told Faith, the gash he'd gotten today was fairly substantial and it hurt like the dickens.

She rolled the sleeve to his shoulder and gasped. There it was, then, the same reaction Susie had had the first time she'd looked upon her husband's scarred body.

He knew what he'd see when he saw Faith's expression—horror and revulsion. Morbid curiosity followed by disgust.

So he didn't look.

He kept his head low and his gaze averted. How had she managed to talk him into this, anyway? He could clean his own wounds at his own house, secure and isolated.

Alone.

And yet here he was, under Faith's gentle ministrations, hating every moment of it but conversely not so much.

She made an exclamation, but it wasn't shock. It was compassion. "You poor thing."

"What?" Her response wasn't what he'd expected at all, and it took him a moment to recover. Was it pity he was hearing?

Anger welled in his chest, and he grasped at it, needing it to cover everything else he was feeling. He didn't want her to feel sorry for him. He didn't want her sympathy.

Her reaction was at least as bad, maybe worse, than her turning away in revulsion, because it jabbed at his insides and made him *feel* things. At least he'd learned how to shield himself to those who turned away at his physical scars.

This, he was defenseless against.

With effort, he hardened his heart. His shoulders tightened with strain. He would not give in.

"I know it hurts, but try not to tense up on me," she gently coaxed. "If you can, try to distract your mind with something." Squinting, she examined the wound, her bottom lip caught in her teeth.

He stared at her full lips so he didn't have to meet her gaze. That was distracting enough for him. He knew by now that biting her lip was a sure sign she was fully concentrating on something, but right now it annoyed him.

She didn't have to be so cute about it. He had plenty to keep his mind on that had nothing to do with the pretty lady tending to his wound—the two babies in his arms, for instance. But no matter how he tried, his babies weren't distracting him, and he didn't like it one bit.

"This has to hurt. How did it happen?"

His fists tightened involuntarily, and he lost his hold on Violet's bottle. He scrambled to readjust, but the bottle rolled from his grasp. Without a word, Faith retrieved it for him, smiling softly as she pressed the container back into his hand. Her gaze shifted from Violet's eyes to his.

She was asking about his scars.

No one asked about his scars. They stared. Gaped. Whispered.

But no one asked.

Where did he even start? And did he want to get into this with her at all?

"I feel so bad about this. I saw Fuego connect with your shoulder, but I didn't see him bite you." Her tone sounded as if she was going to go reprimand the stallion for his bad behavior. "There's no doubt about it, though. I can clearly see the bite marks."

Huh? His mind fogged. What was she talking about?

He'd been thinking about the hideous scar that covered his upper arm all the way to his collarbone. They'd had to graft his skin, and he'd been in the hospital for a long time. It wasn't pretty to look at.

There was some irony in that. As a teenager and young adult he'd never given a thought to his appearance, except for the cocky, youthful knowledge that he was considered attractive by the girls. Now he was suddenly hypersensitive to Faith's eyes on his ugliness.

"He caught me on his way out," Jax explained, still wondering why they were talking about the bite and not his scar. "I was mostly able to roll away from him, but he still managed to take a chunk out of my arm."

"I'll say. I don't think you'll need stitches, but you probably ought to have your doctor take a look at you just to be on the safe side."

He scoffed and shook his head. "I have

every confidence that you can patch me up just fine."

She tore open a couple of packages of alcohol swabs and laid out some gauze.

"This is going to hurt," she warned him.

He set his jaw and didn't flinch when she gently dabbed the alcohol on his skin.

"Sorry. I know it's painful. This is the worst of it, though. I just want to make sure I clean the wound well so there's no chance of infection."

"I can handle it. I'm a big boy." He was too tough to let a little swab get the best of him, even if it was drenched in liquid fire. He tried to smile but grimaced instead.

She laughed, which somehow put him at ease. "No argument there. They grow men large out here in Texas." She spread a big glob of antibacterial ointment over the wound, covered it with gauze and then ran the one-inch-wide self-sticking elastic tape around his biceps several more times than Jax thought was necessary. A little more and he'd practically have a cast.

"Are you current on your rabies vaccine?" she teased.

He snorted. "Fuego had better be the one worried about that."

She laughed as she took Violet from his

arms and settled herself on the burnt-orange sofa across from him. She shifted the baby to her shoulder and gently patted her back.

"I'm sorry my horse went after you that way," she said, her smile faltering. "And after you came over here specifically to help me with him. I can't believe he bit you."

"I won't press charges."

She swept in a surprised breath, and her gaze widened. She looked as startled as if he'd just slapped her.

"You wouldn't—"

"No, of course not," he hastened to say. "I was just kidding. It's not the first time a horse has charged me, and I'm sure it won't be the last. I didn't mean to upset you."

"You didn't. I'm sorry. It's been a really tough day for me and I'm probably overreacting. It's just that Fuego is on his third strike."

"His what?"

"If he doesn't work out here he'll be put down. That's why your remark shocked me so much."

He caught her gaze and held it steady. "You don't ever have to worry about me, Faith. Trust me. I would never do anything to purposefully hurt you or put your rescue in jeopardy. How did Fuego get himself in so much trouble, anyway?"

She shrugged. "I don't know all the details. Probably displaying much of the same behavior as he did today. Possibly acting aggressive." She pinched her lips into a hard line. "I don't want anything to happen to him, but I can't keep a horse who poses a threat to the rest of my herd, or to people who visit the rescue."

She looked so brokenhearted that Jax's gut flipped like a pancake, soaring up, over and then right back down onto the hot griddle. What she lacked in know-how she more than made up for in heart and determination.

"He's not a bad horse. He's a wild stallion. Aggression is to be expected. And I suspect he may not have had great experiences where people are concerned."

Faith nodded and straightened her shoulders. "I was afraid of that."

"Being wild and being gentle aren't mutually exclusive, you know. Would you like me to help you with Fuego?"

Her eyebrows rose, and her eyes gleamed with unshed tears. "Even though he took a chomp out of your shoulder?"

"Especially because he got his teeth into me," he assured her. "It's not just visitors to the rescue that I'm worried about. What if he does something to hurt you? I'll do whatever it takes to keep that from happening."

Relief flooded her gaze. "I feel like I owe you more than I can ever repay. You've done so much for me. And you keep offering."

"Goes both ways. You helped me get on my feet when Rose and Violet got dumped on my doorstep," he reminded her. "Besides—you bought me, remember? Five hundred dollars, I think it was. That's a lot of man-hours."

She chuckled wryly. "I don't own you, Jax."

He grinned.

Maybe she didn't own him, at least not in the technical sense of the word. But he still wanted to help her, protect her and see her dreams come true. And in a way, wasn't that the same thing?

Faith's strategy—staying as far away from Jax and his babies as possible—was failing miserably. In the three weeks since Fuego took a chunk out of Jax's shoulder, Jax had used his training as an excuse to visit her ranch nearly every day, often bringing his daughters along with him.

Faith's favorite times were when his mother, Alice, accompanied him. Faith and Alice would sit and visit and take care of the twins while they watched Jax run Fuego through his paces. Without so much as a lunge lead, he encouraged Fuego to run around the perimeter of the corral, keeping him trotting as much as possible. Faith didn't really understand the process, but Alice assured her she'd get it when Jax was finished.

Honestly, she didn't really care how long Jax took. She enjoyed sitting on the porch, rocking the babies on one of the dual rocking chairs Jax had bought for Faith under the guise of needing to make sure his mother was comfortable. Faith knew it was as much for her as for his mother's ease.

Alice regaled Faith with stories about Jax and his brothers when they were growing up. Not surprisingly, they'd been a handful, getting in trouble in turn and sometimes all three together.

Alice beamed whenever she spoke of her family. She was proud of all her sons. She couldn't say enough good things about Jax's gift with horses. And then there was Slade's bull-riding achievements and Nick's dedication to the ranch. Sometimes she even spoke of Jenson, her late husband.

Jax had shared with Faith how much of a hit his mom had taken when Jenson had passed away after a forty-eight-year marriage. The once-social woman had hidden away in her home and had stopped attending community functions.

Seeing Alice's bubbly and outgoing personality, it was hard to imagine her under the heavy cloud of depression, but Faith knew just how hard grief could hit a person, taking her completely off guard and off grid.

Alice really was a lovely woman. Faith was grateful that Rose and Violet had brought new light into the woman's life and knew that Alice was good for the babies, as well.

"He's amazing," Faith said, watching Jax run the stallion around the corral. "When he started, Fuego wouldn't come within twenty feet of him. Now look at them."

The horse was still skittish, but every day seemed to bring Jax one step closer.

"You haven't seen the half of it," his mother assured her. "He'll have that stallion literally eating out of his hand before he is through. Right now he's teaching the horse to trust him—his scent, his movements, his voice."

She wondered if Alice was aware of the heat that crept up Faith's face at those words. If she did, she was too nice of a person to show it.

Fuego wasn't the only one who responded to Jax's leathery scent, his smooth, muscular movements and that *voice*.

Every time she looked into the depths of his dark, chocolate eyes, all the promises she'd made to herself before moving to Serendipity just whisked away like dandelion seeds on a breezy Texas afternoon.

She knew all the reasons why a relationship with Jax McKenna could never be, but there were an increasing number of moments when it would have been all too easy to set reason aside.

She was grateful for the babies. They were good, natural interruptions that kept things light between her and Jax. And she needed all the help she could get.

After Jax was satisfied with Fuego's progress, it would probably be better if he stopped coming by to check on her entirely, but she would miss Alice. And the babies.

And Jax.

When Fuego was settled, there would no longer be a reason he needed to come by. With a donation she'd received from a recent benefactor, she had been able to hire a couple of teenage wranglers—two girls who came highly recommended by Jax and were especially good with horses. The kids had to balance their ranch work with their schoolwork, but Faith thought it was the perfect solution to a very messy problem.

"Jax was my quiet one," Alice said, smiling softly at the memory. She rhythmically patted Violet's back with each creak of the rocker. "He's the middle child, you know.

"Nick is the textbook firstborn—walks the straight and narrow, strives for perfection in everything he does and really puts his heart into it."

She chuckled. "Slade bothered Nick to no end before he found his way to God and really started growing up. His best friend, Brody, was killed while bull riding, God rest his soul. Such a terrible loss, but I think it forced Slade to take a hard look at his life in a way that he needed." She frowned and shook off the memory. "Slade is settled down now—at least as much as a man like Slade will ever be."

Alice appeared to be meandering in her thoughts. Even though Faith was most curious about Jax, she let Alice continue at her own pace.

"And Jax? He's always been about the horses he trains. He helps Nick with the cattle and daily chores around the ranch, of course, but I think if he had his way, he'd sleep in the stable. Even more so now that—"

She paused. Her gaze darkened. Alice's bottom jaw jutted out under her top one for a moment as she struggled to regain her composure. At length, the older woman scoffed and shook her head.

"I'm sorry, but when I think about what *that woman* did to my son, it makes me angry enough to spit nails. If ever there was a woman set out to try my temper, it is *that woman*." She wouldn't even say Susie's name.

Faith didn't want to pry, but clearly Alice needed to talk about it. She prayed she'd be a good sounding board and that Alice would realize she was trustworthy.

"You mean Susie? Are you talking about the way she dumped the twins on him?"

"Well, yes, there're the girls, of course. There is no excuse for that but—"

Faith didn't realize Jax had stopped calling and nickering to the stallion until he strode to the fence and braced one foot on the bottom rung, leaving Fuego to his own devices on the far side of the corral.

"You're staring at me," he accused, lifting his hat by the crown and wiping the sweat from his brow with the fabric at the bottom of his T-shirt. "Are you two talking about me?"

"I was just about to show Faith your baby pictures," Alice teased. "I've already told her lots of stories about you."

Scorching heat flooded straight to Faith's

cheeks. Jax caught her gaze and he raised one eyebrow. Silence stretched between them for what seemed like forever. Her heart pounded so furiously she thought he might be able to hear it.

Then he grinned, that heart-flipping half smile yanked up by his scar. And he winked at her.

Winked.

While Alice was sitting right there in their midst. His mother had surely seen the exchange.

Just when Faith thought the level of her mortification could rise no further, Jax found a way to increase it. Her head was likely to pop off from the pressure of the heat between her ears.

"All good things, I hope." He included his mother with his statement and the wide grin that accompanied it. "I would hate to think you were talking trash about me."

"I've been telling her what little terrors you and your brothers were when you were children. These gray hairs?" She pointed to her shoulder-length hair, still a deep black spun with shades of silver. "Every single one of them has your names on it. Nick. Jax. Slade." She pointed them out one by one. "You're blessed, young man," she continued, wagging a finger at Jax. "You have daughters."

Jax threw back his head and laughed. Faith smiled. It was the most carefree she'd ever heard him. He was always so tense, and with good reason. She was glad he could loosen up around his mother.

Fuego neighed and snorted.

"I'd best get back to the stallion. No rest for the wicked, right?"

Alice scoffed. "Don't let him fool you," she informed Faith. "He's a good man, that one, right to the core. He has a heart of gold, broken though it is. He just needs the right woman to mend it up for him."

Alice looked directly at Faith and raised her eyebrows.

Asking? Insinuating?

Faith cleared her suddenly tight throat and swallowed hard to relieve the pressure.

To distract herself, she laid a plastic pad across her lap and made a big production out of changing Rose's diaper.

Alice was still peering at her inquisitively. What in the world did Jax's mom expect her to say?

She knew what she *should* say.

I'm not interested in Jax in that way.

Well, that would be an outright lie, because how could she not be interested?

There's nothing between us.

Still not quite right. After what had happened the day Fuego had taken a bite out of Jax, she could hardly say they hadn't shared anything emotional. And the chemistry was undeniable.

There will never be anything serious between Jax and me because I won't ever let there be.

It was as close to the truth as she was going to get in her confused state of mind.

It was also something she could never tell Jax's mother.

"Susie was Jax's high school sweetheart." Alice picked up the thread of the conversation as if she'd never left it. "You know how it is in a small-town ranching community. Since most of the kids already know what they are doing with their lives, those who pair up tend to stay that way—after high school they marry off and have families right away.

"Susie wasn't like that. She had aspirations that went beyond Serendipity. Which was okay, in theory. She went away to college while Jax remained home tending the family ranch."

Alice shook her head, remembering. "When

Susie returned to Serendipity, she was a different girl. Worldly and bitter. Life hadn't quite worked out the way she'd anticipated. She didn't ever get her degree. I don't know what she was doing all that time away.

"Whatever she got into, it changed her, and not for the better. The only one who couldn't see it was Jax. Or maybe he was just set on honoring his commitment to her. You know how Jax is. Honestly, what I can't figure out is why Susie married him. She was never happy, even before…" Alice's sentence trailed off.

"Before the accident?"

Alice pressed her lips and nodded. Her gaze flickered to Jax and then back to Faith again. "Jax should probably be the one telling you this, but he'll never do it and I don't believe he can move on until he gets past the tragedy of what happened. And that's not likely to occur if no one besides his own family knows what truly went down that night."

Faith was at once honored and terrified that Alice had bestowed on her the gift of her trust. She knew the woman wasn't giving it lightly, not when it had to do with her son.

"He told me he was injured in an accident, but he never said any more than that."

"He doesn't like to talk about it. He was returning to Serendipity from watching Slade compete in an out-of-town rodeo. He'd asked Susie to accompany him, but she no longer cared for *country* activities. She'd seen how the other half lived, apparently, and wanted Jax to move to the city."

Faith kissed Rose's downy head and watched Jax work, his strength and confidence matching the stallion's. It was hard to believe that a vulnerable heart beat in that big old chest of his, a heart that could be injured by one thoughtless woman's words and deeds. But she'd glimpsed enough of Jax to know how badly Susie had hurt him.

"On the highway on his way home, a car in front of him blew out a tire and went headlong into a tree. Jax immediately pulled to the side of the road and called 911, then rushed to see if he could help. You know Jax. He's not the kind of man to stand around and do nothing."

That sounded exactly like the Jax Faith knew.

"The driver had hit her head and was barely conscious, so he wrapped his jacket around his arm and broke a window out and then dragged the woman and her six-year-old son to safety."

Faith gasped, then frowned in confusion. The jagged scar on his face might possibly have been caused by a sharp piece of glass, but his shoulder told another story.

"What happened to his arm? That doesn't look like an injury consistent with a wound caused by sharp glass. I'd have guessed it was a burn scar."

Her eyes grew wide. "You're right—it is from a burn. I have to say, I'm surprised he showed you his arm. It's one of his big secrets."

She sniffed. "Oh, believe me, he didn't want me to see it. I kind of forced the issue. Fuego took a bite out of his shoulder, and I insisted that I be the one to patch him up, since it was my fault it happened."

"Still…" Alice stopped her rhythmic patting on Violet's back and tilted her head, analyzing Faith. "He's very sensitive about that scar."

"It doesn't bother me. Honestly. But I'm curious. How'd he get burned?"

"The car was on fire when he went to rescue the woman and her child. He went back to make sure there weren't any other people left in the car. The driver had been dazed and kept saying something about her baby— turned out later that she meant the six-year-old, but Jax believed another child might still be caught in the wreck."

"There wasn't, I hope."

"No. But the engine exploded before Jax could clear away. The car rolled with him in it. He was badly burned and had to have skin grafts on his shoulder. And he lost most of the hearing in his left ear, you know."

Faith hoped Alice didn't hear her gasp. Jax was deaf in one ear. That explained a lot. "Praise God he's still alive to tell the story."

"Indeed."

Faith reached out to squeeze Alice's hand. The poor woman had been through so much recently. First she had lost her husband, and then the near death of her son so soon afterward. What a nightmare. It certainly put Faith's meager problems in perspective.

"Come on, boy." Jax's deep, lyrical voice reached Faith's ears, and she turned to watch him. "Get up, now. Show me what you're made of."

"He rescued those people. He's a hero," she whispered.

Alice nodded. "Everyone thinks so but him."

"I don't understand. He threw himself in harm's way for people he didn't even know. In my book that makes him a Good Samaritan, and he has the scars to prove it. How could he think any differently?"

"He hates those scars."

"But—why?" It wasn't even that she respected the scars now that she knew the story behind the wounds, that he had been performing an act of mercy when he received them. Even before she'd known what caused them, the scars hadn't bothered her. Particularly that jagged scar on his temple. Hadn't anyone ever told him it gave him a rugged, bad-boy appearance? Women ate up the tough-guy image. She had to believe she was not the only one who thought Jax McKenna was a good-looking man.

Alice snorted. "In a word—Susie. She completely shattered his self-image. On the day the doctor removed his bandages, she took one look at Jax and walked out of his life. Poof. She was gone. He came home from the hospital to an empty house. Susie had cleaned out her drawers and taken most everything of value. Divorce papers followed a week later."

"A *week*?" Faith was aghast.

"Right? If you ask me, those divorce papers were in the works well before the accident happened."

"Clearly."

"But Jax doesn't see it. To him, his scars ruined his marriage. He looks in the mirror and he sees himself as a monster. So he hides himself away at the ranch, trying to make the outside world go away. As if it ever does." She sighed and paused to deposit a now-sleeping Violet into her car seat.

Rose was still fussing, so Faith continued to rock her, receiving as much comfort from the rhythmic motion as she was giving to the baby.

"He rarely goes into town for any reason other than to attend church, and even then he never stays to socialize. The Bachelors and Baskets auction was actually the first community event he's attended since his injury."

That was odd. "Pardon me for saying so, Alice, but why did he choose that one? If he doesn't like being on display, putting himself up on an auction block for everyone to see would be his worst nightmare."

"Believe me—it was. At least until you stepped up with the winning bid and rescued him out of his misery. He was your first official wild rescue." Alice smiled at her joke but quickly sobered. "You see, his father passed away in a hospice in San Antonio. He needed round-the-clock care and there simply wasn't a closer facility. The boys took turns driving me back and forth to see Jenson, and it was hard on all of us. Nick missed his father's passing, and he's never forgiven himself for that. Jax and Slade were there, but that didn't make it easier for either one of them. If there had been a hospice here in Serendipity—well, that would have changed everything."

Faith nodded.

"So you see, Jax would do anything for the cause—even put himself on display."

"That was very brave of him. I can't even begin to imagine the pure torture he must have been feeling, standing up there on that grandstand. He probably thought everyone was looking at his scar."

"Interesting how our perspective changes based on where we are sitting, isn't it? Now that I think about it, I suppose I've done the same thing I've accused Jax of doing. After Jenson died, I retreated to the ranch because of my broken heart."

"That's understandable, Alice," Faith assured her. "Everyone grieves differently."

Different perspectives.

Faith had grieved by running away to the country and hiding out among her mustangs.

"Well, the twins have certainly shaken things up around here." Alice laughed, a clear, happy sound that made Faith smile.

"That's one way of looking at it. Your family's whole worldview has shifted. But from what I've seen, Jax is handling it tremendously well. He's definitely daddy material. Those girls are blessed to have him, and anyone can tell how much he loves them."

"I can't say I mind spoiling these two little sweethearts myself. They make my heart sing. The way all this came down on us was definitely less than ideal, but in this case it's the end result that matters. Rose and Violet have a family who loves them. Jax will give them a good, stable Christian home. All of us will."

Faith sighed inwardly. If only every child was so blessed as to have a man like Jax for a father. Her own dad had been more interested in climbing the corporate ladder than in praying with his only daughter before she climbed into bed for the night.

"When Jax finishes gentling Fuego, we'll have to have a party to celebrate," Alice announced, with so much excitement in her tone that Faith knew she wasn't going to turn Jax's mom down, whatever she offered. "Dinner at my house. We'll raise a toast to Jax for his labor, but you and I both know it will be for much more than that. We'll be celebrating his courage and his future with his two beautiful daughters."

Alice looked as if she was about to say

more, but then she abruptly closed her mouth and shook her head.

"You'll come, won't you?" she asked after an extended pause.

"Yes, of course." Faith tried to smile but it felt shaky at best.

She would show up and do her best to look happy, but she wouldn't be celebrating the end of Jax's work with Fuego—she'd be grieving the loss of his friendship.

Because she couldn't continue to be friends with Jax McKenna. Not without getting her heart woven up with him and the twins. And that was something she simply could not allow herself to do.

The party had given her an extension—a few more days to spend with Jax, assuming he continued to show up at her ranch—but she wouldn't let herself think beyond that.

"Look there," Alice said, nodding toward the corral. "This is what he's been waiting for. Watch."

Jax slowed Fuego's pace and then turned his back on the horse. He stood stock-still in the middle of the corral, his arms hanging loosely at his sides and a confident, expectant look on his face.

Faith held her breath. She had no idea what

would happen next, but she instinctively knew it would be beautiful, a moment to savor.

Fuego snorted and threw his head, stepping toward Jax and then bucking and backing up again, turning indecisively in a tight circle.

Still, Jax did not move.

"Come on, Fuego," Alice whispered, leaning forward in her chair.

Tentatively, the stallion started back toward Jax, and this time he did not startle or turn away. He stopped just behind Jax and sniffed at his neck and shoulder, nickering as if accepting the man's scent as trustworthy.

"That's my boy," Jax murmured, turning with a slow, even motion and running a reassuring hand down the horse's muzzle. "See now? Everything is okay."

He continued to stroke Fuego's head and neck, speaking in the lyrical voice that mesmerized horses and humans alike, as butterflies fluttered through her stomach.

Amazing.

Jax was simply amazing.

Faith's heart welled. His patience with the wild stallion had paid off in spades. Without so much as a halter, Fuego willingly followed Jax to the gate that emptied out into the front meadow, nickering when Jax opened it.

"Go on now, boy," Jax said, running his

hand down the horse's neck one last time. "Your band is waiting for you."

What Faith had just witnessed was beyond anything she could have imagined when she had first conceived of rescuing horses. Jax had opened a whole new world to her.

She wanted to thank him but knew he'd act as if what he'd done was just another day's work. He strode up to the porch two steps at a time and took Rose in his arms, nuzzling her neck and making her pump her arms and gurgle in delight.

"Fuego will be approachable now." He smiled, and for once Faith didn't see a shadow of pain in his eyes.

"Amazing." Faith could find her voice for only the one word. She had a hundred words in her head, but they were all verses of the same song.

"That's my son," Alice agreed, a proud smile splitting her face. "Absolutely amazing. It looks like we're going to have that celebratory dinner sooner than we expected."

Jax's eyebrow rose. "What are we celebrating, or do I want to know?"

Alice flashed a wink at Faith and smiled at Jax. "Why, you, of course."

Chapter Six

Amazing.

If Jax heard that word one more time, he was going to knock his head against a wall. The day he'd finished Fuego, Faith had repeated the compliment at least five times that he'd counted.

Every day for the rest of the week he'd been working at her ranch, and he'd heard it over and over again.

Amazing, amazing, amazing.

Good grief. The woman couldn't get over it.

His mom was not helping. She had come through on her threat to throw a celebratory dinner over the weekend. He suspected it was more for Faith than it was for him, though his mom said otherwise. He had a close family, but they didn't get together every time one of them did something worthwhile.

He hated the thought that he was going to end up the focus of the evening. It made him itchy all over to think about what fun his brothers were going to have with all this. He'd never hear the end of it. And on top of their teasing, he still had to deal with Faith's praise.

All he'd done was gentle her stallion. She was acting as if he'd flown her to the moon and back.

He smiled. He had to admit she was good for his ego. She seemed genuinely appreciative of the work he'd done around her ranch, especially with Fuego. That was probably part of the reason he kept going back. She asked a lot of questions, sometimes curious, always learning—so many queries that he would definitely have been annoyed by them if they'd come from anyone but her.

Faith was different.

Most telling of all, she didn't seem to be the least bit put off by his scarred body. After the afternoon she'd patched up his shoulder when Fuego bit him, she'd never mentioned his injuries again, and it hadn't changed their relationship at all. If anything, it had brought them closer.

Sometimes—sometimes—he thought he caught her staring, but it wasn't the way others gawked at him.

Her gaze was sweet. Tender. It made his gut feel all fluttery. He wondered...

His chest tightened. He was reading too much into a simple look. Faith wasn't good at shielding her emotions, which was good, because in general he was lousy at reading them. Even though she never talked about it, he knew she had her own issues from her past.

Could she get beyond them?

Could he?

No.

Those thoughts were leading him down a path he could not afford to tread, not only because Susie had trampled on his heart and left it in shreds by the roadside, but because his focus needed to remain entirely concentrated on raising his daughters.

On the other hand, it was true that Faith wasn't anything like Susie.

He trusted Faith implicitly. She would never belittle anyone for any reason. And she was a wonder with the twins. Sometimes he'd covertly watch her with one of the babies and wonder why she wasn't married with a family of her own. She obviously loved kids.

Maybe that was part of the grief she carried in her eyes. He wouldn't pry, but he hoped he'd proved she could count on his friendship. If she ever wanted to open up to him, he would listen.

Faith was the first guest to arrive at the house, bearing two pies that she promptly admitted she did not bake. Phoebe Hawkins at Cup O' Jo's Café in town was a world-class baker.

"I don't even want to try to compete with that," Faith said, laughing. She set the pies on the sideboard and turned to Jax.

He chuckled. "My mom ordered our chicken from the deli. She likes to say, 'Why should I slave away in a hot kitchen when there're so many other nice things to do?' But the truth is, cooking is not her forte."

"I'm with her on that. Besides, I'm too busy with the horses to mess around with culinary endeavors. And my kitchen isn't exactly well equipped. The appliances aren't in very good shape. Now, what can I do to help you?"

"Um—set the silverware, I guess."

Jax had the oddest sensation that the atmosphere of the house had lightened the moment Faith walked in. Maybe it was because of the way her smile seemed to brighten up any room she entered. Maybe it was knowing he could be himself around her without worrying about what he was saying or doing, or that she was staring at him for all the wrong reasons.

He was, after all, *amazing*.

He grinned. Whatever it was, he liked it. She made him feel less burdened. More secure. He couldn't wipe the smile from his face if he tried.

Which was kindling for a very large fire. He might as well just hand Nick and Slade a pack of matches and be done with it. They were going to take one look at his face and off they'd go, razzing him to no end, assuming there was something romantic going on between him and Faith.

And worse yet, they would give Faith a whole lot of the same kind of trouble.

For his part, he could handle it. He'd been picked on enough growing up with his two rough-and-tumble brothers that there was nothing they could say or do to ruffle him. But how fair was that to Faith? She didn't deserve the ribbing that was most certainly coming her way. He was pretty sure she didn't want to hear his brothers' teasing suggestions about romance or anything else.

Jax was so busy worrying about what his brothers could or would say that he didn't notice how many pieces of his mother's best silverware Faith had laid out at each place setting.

"Whoa, whoa, whoa there, cowgirl," he said, throwing up his hands. "How many forks does one man need to eat his meal?"

Three, apparently. At least Faith thought so.

She looked at him in dismay. "I was just trying to make it look fancy. Do you think it's too much, then?"

"Believe me—one knife, one fork and one spoon is all we'll be needing," he advised her with a smile. "Any more than that and my brothers will take to creating such a ruckus over it that you'll never hear the end of it."

Alice entered the room, wiping her hands on a dish towel. "Why, Faith dear, I didn't hear you come in."

"She brought pies," Jax said, patting his lean middle.

"Phoebe's pies," Faith qualified.

"The table looks lovely, honey," she said, addressing Jax. "I especially like what you've done with the silverware." Alice flashed Jax a crafty smile before returning to the kitchen. The Cheshire cat couldn't have done a better job of it. Jax thought he might even have caught a wink.

Jax met Faith's eyes, and they broke into smothered laughter.

"Guess we're keeping the silverware," Faith said, covering her mouth with her palm as another giggle escaped.

Jax shook his head. "Don't say I didn't warn you. There will be a food fight before the night is over."

"Don't worry about me. I can take anything your brothers sling at me. Even peas. And I give as good as I get."

He choked on his laughter. She probably could, Jax realized. Maybe his brothers ought to be the ones to look out. Faith was strong and sure of herself, able to take life as it came to her. But that didn't mean he wasn't going to do his best to shelter her from the worst of the familial fallout.

The doorbell rang repeatedly, as if someone was holding the button down. Jax's first thought was of his sleeping babies, followed by thunderous intentions toward whichever idiot brother thought ringing the doorbell was a good idea.

Somebody's head was going to roll.

"I'll get it," Faith said. "You'd better check on the twins."

Jax growled in agreement and crept down the hallway, gingerly avoiding the loose floorboards that creaked when he stepped on them, like a soldier in a minefield. He'd often stayed at his mother's during those first few crucial days with his girls. Long nights pacing the hallway had taught him where each and every creak and squeak was located.

He peeked into the portable crib, where Rose and Violet were napping. Happily, the doorbell hadn't wakened either baby. He wanted them to get as much rest as possible before chaos reigned supreme in the house.

He watched Violet sleep for a moment, measuring the rise and fall of her chest and smiling softly at her sweet little face and the way she sucked noisily on her fist in her sleep.

Happy dreams, little ones.

He tiptoed out of the room and closed the door so it was open only a crack. His mother had installed a baby monitor, but he was still in that first-time parent freak-out-at-the-tiniest-little-noise phase, which his mother often teased him about.

So he was a little overprotective. He wasn't sure he would *ever* get over that phase. Look out, teenage boys wanting to date either one of his daughters.

Still grinning, he turned the corner of the hallway into the family room, where Faith was standing at the front door, her mouth agape.

"Jax?" she squeaked in a high, tight voice.

He immediately went on full alert, adrenaline shooting through his veins. Faith's defensive posture and the fact that she was literally blocking the doorway was a clear signal that it wasn't one of his brothers standing there, but who—

"Jackson?" a shrill voice called, sending a chill down Jax's spine. "This *woman* will not let me in the house. Tell her to get out of my way. I want to see my babies."

At the sound of Susie's voice, every muscle in Jax's body tightened to the point of pain, but the angry haze in his mind made him oblivious to it.

This was *so* not happening. And if she thought she was going to waltz in and see the twins, she was highly mistaken.

Faith, bless her courageous little heart, hadn't budged from where she blocked the doorway. The set of her shoulders suggested she wasn't taking this unwanted invasion any better than he was, but she was tough and determined and he was glad he had her fighting on his side—on his children's side.

Forcing himself to take a deep breath, he moved into the doorway behind Faith and laid a reassuring hand on her shoulder.

Calm. Cool. Collected.

He'd been fervently praying to be able to forgive Susie for all of her thoughtless actions, but then the second he saw her face it all came rushing back—the humiliation, the pain of rejection. The grief caused by the death of a marriage. The shock when he'd suddenly discovered he was a father twice over and that his babies had been unfeelingly dumped on his front porch.

Surprisingly, though, there was one key emotion missing from the equation. Susie no longer had the ability to break his heart. Not because it was already broken beyond repair, but because it had healed—and it no longer belonged to her. His love for her was truly in the past.

"What are you doing here, Susie?" he demanded. "Circle M isn't your home anymore."

He swept his gaze across his ex-wife. The long brown curls she'd once put so much stock into had lost their bounce and sheen. Her eyes were glassy and the pupils dilated to the point where her normally blue eyes appeared nearly black. Susie had always been slender, but now she looked skeletal. The woman who had always been so particular about her appearance was gone, replaced by a stranger Jax barely recognized.

He narrowed his eyes on her. "You didn't drive here on your own, did you?"

She scowled and crossed her arms, the long orange sleeves of her shirt flopping over her wrists. "So what if I did?"

So what?

She was clearly on something, making driving a vehicle both dangerous and illegal.

She scoffed. "If you must know, my boyfriend, Michael, drove me here. He prefers not to see you, so he's waiting for me in the car." Her scowl deepened. "Don't judge, Jax. You have no idea how difficult it was for me to come here today."

Jax wondered if this Michael fellow was in any better condition to drive than Susie, but he didn't ask. Maybe it was better not to know.

"Come in." Jax sighed and stepped aside, sliding his hand from Faith's shoulder to her waist, keeping her close to his side. As much as he would have liked to believe he was somehow offering her comfort with the physical contact, he knew better.

Faith was his rock.

Jax gestured Susie to the armchair and guided Faith to the couch. He drew her down beside him and rested his arm over the back of the sofa after they sat. To his relief, Faith didn't protest. She seemed to understand that he wanted Susie to know he'd moved on with his life—although probably not as far as Susie might interpret, given Faith's presence and their body language toward each other.

Susie gave Faith a pointed look. "Jax and I need to talk. Alone."

He stiffened and slid his arm firmly around Faith's shoulders. "Faith stays. Anything you have to say to me you can say to both of us."

And to his mother, who was standing just out of sight in the space that separated the family room from the dining room. Jax had seen her when he'd turned around to let Susie in.

He figured she would make her presence known if and when she wanted to, and in the meantime, she had as much a right to hear this conversation as anybody present.

"Make it quick," he said. "My brothers will be here in a few minutes for a family dinner."

"Oh! And how are Nick and Slade?" Susie's voice was animated, sounding as if they were old friends engaged in small talk.

He raised his brows. As if she cared.

"Get to the point." Maybe his voice was a little too abrupt, but what did she expect? He was coping the best he could, given the circumstances.

"Okay." Susie smoothed her palms on her

jeans and pulled her mouth into a pout, an expression that used to work especially well on Jax. Now he felt nothing other than mild annoyance and the urge to roll his eyes.

"Well, then, if we're not going to talk, I'd like to see the babies now." The cavalier way she referred to her children made him sick, and even worse was the way she shifted her gaze to Faith. "Why don't you be a dear and go get them for me?"

"No." He wasn't going to beat around the bush with this, and he wasn't about to give in to her demands. "You are in no condition to see the twins right now."

He was torn. In a perfect world, the twins would be raised by both a mother and a father, and neither parent would ever have to be separated from them. But he had to do what was best for his babies. Even were Susie not as high as a kite, she was still the woman who had had the gall to dump Rose and Violet on his doorstep. He couldn't trust her to be someone whom the twins could count on, and he wouldn't risk hurting them by letting her back into their lives. Not when there was every chance she'd just let them down again.

He suddenly wished Faith was the twins' mother. She would never put her own needs above the girls', and under her gentle guidance his babies would each grow up to become a strong, independent woman, as Faith was.

He didn't even realize he was squeezing her shoulders until she cleared her throat and glanced up at Jax, her gaze silently asking him if it was okay for her to speak.

Of course she should speak her mind. He nodded briefly.

"Honestly, Susie," Faith began, "I think you lost your rights to Rose and Violet the moment you left them on Jax's front porch and walked away."

"Who? And who cares what you think, anyway?" Susie crossed her arms and glared at Faith.

"I care," Jax assured both ladies. "As for the nicknames, we didn't know the twins' names when you left them with us. If you recall, you didn't even bother to include that information. I tried repeatedly to get a hold of you, but you refused to pick up your phone or reply to any of my messages. So we nicknamed them Rose and Violet. They are a good fit for their individual personalities."

"We?" Susie glared at Faith, but Faith didn't respond in kind. She kept her spine erect and her chin high. Jax could feel the

tension in her shoulders, but it didn't show on her face.

"You let some woman nickname *our* babies? Their names," Susie informed them, "are Elaine and Patricia."

"Fine. Elaine and Patricia. Good to know. Birth certificates would be nice." So now he knew the twins' legal names. But he was still going to call the girls Rose and Violet. He couldn't and wouldn't change that now. Their names wouldn't change, and neither would their living situation.

"What *is* your plan?" Faith asked. "For after you see the babies, I mean?"

Susie shrugged. "I haven't thought that far ahead. I guess Michael and I will take them back to our place."

"I see," Faith said drily. "You have cribs? Diapers? Formula? You've babyproofed your home?"

Susie looked unsure of herself. "Well, no. We live in a trailer, but it can't be that hard to—"

"You need plug protectors for every outlet." Jax pushed his advantage. "All of your *medicine*—" he emphasized the word "—has to be locked away."

"All of your cabinets and drawers need child locks," Faith added.

"They're only tiny babies. They can't even crawl yet," she argued. "Why would I need child locks?"

Jax wondered if she still pictured the children as she'd left them. Didn't she realize how much they'd grown in the two months he'd had them? "They can roll over," Jax said proudly, feeling the accomplishment just as strongly as if he'd done it himself. "I do tummy time with them every day, and they are really strong. They can even sit up with help."

"Tummy what?"

Jax wasn't about to go into all the details of child rearing—or any of them, for that matter—because he'd already decided it wasn't in his children's best interest to have Susie in their lives. Not until she'd cleaned up her own life. If that ever happened.

"Did you not read any baby books during your pregnancy?" Faith asked in astonishment.

Susie snorted. "Not that it's any of your business, but I didn't want to be pregnant in the first place. So no, I did not read any baby books."

The pained expression that crossed Jax's face nearly ripped Faith's heart out. He might have been caught completely unaware on the day he found the twins left on his doorstep, but from the very first second, he'd loved those girls with every part of his heart and soul. For him to hear that Susie had never wanted them in the first place…

Since she'd abandoned them, it wasn't a huge stretch for Faith to believe it, but she knew it had to hurt Jax. For his babies' own mother to treat them with such a blasé attitude was beyond the pale for any man.

"I was going to give them up for adoption to some needy couple like you see in the movies," she said, sounding completely juvenile and at the same time self-righteous, as if someone ought to crown her for her thoughtfulness and charity. How far was that from the truth? "But then after I had them I thought it might be kind of fun to be a mom. So I kept them instead."

"But you didn't keep them," Jax reminded her, his jaw clamped so tight he was speaking through his clenched teeth. "You left them on my front porch. What happened, Susie? Motherhood wasn't all you thought it would be? Did it become too inconvenient for you? Were the kids cramping your style?"

His tone was laced with sarcasm, but Faith couldn't blame him for that. His muscles were pulsing, tightening in on themselves, like a cougar ready to spring on its prey.

She laid a gentle hand on his knee, reminding him of her support—and that it wouldn't do any good to argue with Susie. Not in her current state. He appeared to understand her unspoken gesture, taking a deep breath and covering her hand with his own.

"The first day was okay, but after that it got bad. Michael didn't like all the noise. He was complaining constantly, and he wasn't helping me at all. I didn't see why I had to do everything. I figured you have your whole family to help you out."

"And he does," Alice said, suddenly deciding to make her presence known. Faith hadn't actually seen her up to now but had assumed she was somewhere just out of sight, listening in on the conversation. "Those precious girls have us, and they have Faith."

Faith's heart welled. She'd never been included in a family before. When she was growing up, it had just been her and her dad, and he'd never taken much interest in her. She'd spent enough time with Keith's son to fall in love with him, but Keith himself had never introduced her to his parents, which she now realized should have been a glaring neon

sign to her that something was not right—
much like the one Susie was holding up now.

Parts of Susie's story didn't add up. "Wait.
So you want to take the babies back, right?
But you said you're still with Michael."

She shrugged. "I am."

"Then what do you imagine is going to be
different this time around?" Faith's patience
was wearing thin, and she was struggling to
keep a grasp on her temper. The last thing
Jax needed now was for her to come unglued
on him.

"The babies are older, right? Like Jax said.
Almost sitting up and all that? They won't
bawl like they did at first. They'll be easier
to take care of."

"I've got news for you." Jax scoffed. "Babies
cry. Even three-month-olds. That's one of the
primary ways they communicate."

"Oh." Susie pursed her lips.

Jax blew out a breath. His hand slipped underneath Faith's, palm to palm, and he linked
his fingers through hers. She gave his hand a
reassuring squeeze.

"Susie, I've got to be honest with you, and
you need to be honest with yourself. You're in
no condition to care for the twins. You need
some time to figure out your own life. Get
yourself clean."

"But I want to see the babies now. Tonight."

"That's not going to happen." Jax was firm but gentle. Faith admired his self-control. She wasn't sure she would have behaved as well as he was doing. "Not in your present condition. I'm not trying to be unreasonable, but I don't want the children to see you this way."

"They're just babies!" Susie wailed, loud enough to *wake* the babies.

"Nevertheless, this is nonnegotiable."

"I have rights."

"I don't think you do. You gave up your rights the moment you abandoned your children. Your current lifestyle doesn't lend itself to a family. Take a look at yourself. Think about Michael. You two don't want to be burdened with children. I, on the other hand, have a quiet lifestyle and my family's support. The girls need to stay with me. Please don't try to fight me on this."

Faith had to admit Susie looked legitimately crestfallen, the way a child would if her ice cream fell out of her cone and landed on the hot sidewalk. In that moment, she genuinely felt sorry for Susie, who'd somehow strayed far from the path of her youth. Faith prayed she'd find God's redeeming grace.

But Faith was firmly with Jax where the welfare of the babies was concerned. Susie was in no way a fit mother. Not now, possibly not ever.

"If and when you clean up your life, I'll be happy to meet together—just the two of us—and reevaluate how you might fit into the girls' lives. But even then, you have to realize that you'll need to make many changes to accommodate the twins, and I'll have to be sure you're making a permanent commitment to them. No disappearing for months at a time and then suddenly reappearing, deciding you want to play mommy again. It's not fair to the girls for their emotions to be jerked around like that, and I'll not allow it."

Faith's heart turned over. Big, strong Jax at his best, protecting his two little sweethearts, who had become his world. He'd learned how to feed them, change them, wash them and rock them to sleep, but the most important thing of all—loving them—he hadn't had to learn. He'd done it from the start.

Clearly there was nothing left to say to Susie, so Jax stood and pulled Faith to her feet, keeping hold of her hand. Susie also stood and stepped in front of Jax, gazing up at him with a mixture of sadness, resentment and contempt in her expression.

Her brow lowered and she lifted a hand, tracing her finger down the scar on Jax's face.

He shuddered. Faith tightened her grip on his hand.

Susie still has the power to get to him.

Of course she did. He'd been married to her for years, and it hadn't been his decision to split with her. His heart was probably breaking all over again, and looking at his miserable expression, Faith's heart broke for him.

She cared for Jax, probably a great deal more than she should, and she didn't like seeing him hurt.

"I think it's time for you to leave now." Faith's voice held an edge to it, and her proverbial claws sprang out. She'd had enough of *that woman* for one evening.

Susie's gaze flashed to her and she scoffed. "Excuse me?"

She might still have some influence over Jax, but if Susie thought she was going to intimidate Faith, she had another thing coming.

Susie turned back to Jax. "Honestly, I don't know how your little girlfriend here can even stand to look at you."

Jax looked as if he'd been slapped. Faith couldn't believe the woman could be so intentionally hurtful. She grabbed Susie's elbow and none too gently turned her toward the door.

"Go. Now," she demanded.

Susie tried to jerk her arm away, but Faith held it tight until they reached the door. She was just reaching for the handle when the door opened from the outside, nearly plowing both women down.

Nick, Slade, his wife, Laney, and their toddler, Brody, barreled in the door, talking and laughing, their arms laden with food.

Nick and Slade froze in shocked silence when they realized Susie was in the room.

"What's *she* doing here?" Nick growled.

Faith waited a moment for Jax to respond, but he didn't appear to be able to find his voice.

"Susie was just leaving," Faith informed them, ushering her through the open doorway and watching until she and Michael drove out of sight.

When Faith turned around, she realized everyone's eyes were on her. Heat flared to her cheeks. She had no right to tell anyone to come or go. This wasn't her house, nor was it even her fight.

Suddenly the room burst into spontaneous applause.

"Well done," Slade cheered. "Way to put Susie in her place."

The protective gleam that Faith had so often seen in Jax's eyes was now reflected in his brothers' expressions, and she decided she liked them very much.

"I don't know," she said, dropping her gaze. She really hadn't done anything special.

"I do." Jax's usually clear voice was husky.

The monitor crackled to life with the sound of hungry, babbling babies. Jax and Faith looked at each other and laughed, the tension broken.

"Shall we?" Jax smiled and offered his arm to her. Her heart inflated and her stomach felt giddy.

Laney cleared her throat, and the room burst into action. Chatter resumed as Jax's brothers moved into the dining room with their offerings for the party.

Jax and Faith walked in companionable silence to the nursery Alice had set up in her spare room.

Faith was lost in her thoughts—or rather, her feelings. She was trying to contain the quivering that came after an adrenaline rush. She was greatly relieved that the whole ordeal was over—for tonight, at least. She was sad that it would never really be over for Jax and the children. And—

Jax whirled around so suddenly that she nearly walked into him.

"Faith, before we go in and get the babies,

I—I just want to tell you—" He paused and swept in a ragged breath, his Adam's apple bobbing. "That is, I—"

His lips were on hers before she knew what was happening. Soft, warm, sweet. His reassuring scent wrapped around her senses, a heady combination of leather and the countryside that was uniquely Jax.

His fingers threaded through her hair, drawing her nearer, while his other arm stole around her waist. He groaned her name and slanted his head, deepening the kiss, and she wrapped her arms around his neck, welcoming him into her heart.

After a minute Rose's babble became a wail, and Jax broke off the kiss, leaning his forehead against hers, their breaths mingling.

"I have to—" he started, then kissed her again.

She smiled into his lips. "I know. Go. I'm right behind you."

He brushed his palm down her cheek.

"No," he whispered softly. "You're not behind me, sweetheart. You're right by my side, and for that I'm eternally grateful."

Chapter Seven

Sunday morning, Jax attended church with his family. Faith was there, but she stayed chatting within a crowd of single women until the service was ready to begin, and then she sat on the opposite side of the sanctuary.

Little more than an awkward smile had passed between them the whole morning. The atmosphere wasn't companionable between them as it had always been before. She wouldn't even look him in the eye, and he had no doubt she was avoiding him.

He just didn't know why.

Thanks to Susie's inopportune visit, the celebratory dinner had been a little less animated than it might have otherwise been. His mother, Faith and Laney had tried their best to redirect the atmosphere and the conversation, mostly citing all the exciting things that were happening at Untamed—the repairs on the outbuildings, Faith's ever-growing herd and Jax's success gentling Fuego.

Jax appreciated the women's efforts to make things better, but he couldn't shake his myriad thoughts, which were traveling at the speed of light with a variety of emotions tagged to their backs.

He'd known Susie would return some day, asking for the kids, but he hadn't been prepared for it to be so soon. Susie was a loose cannon. He would never know when she might appear to shoot things down again. He was just getting used to having his daughters here, and Susie could potentially ruin that.

And now he feared Susie had somehow damaged his relationship with Faith. Or was it the kiss they'd shared that was the reason she was avoiding him? But that left a lot of questions, and he knew the only way to get answers was to go to Faith and ask her straight-out what was bothering her.

Whatever she was feeling, he wanted to reassure her that last night's kiss wasn't a fluke. He needed time to put his head and heart in order, but if she was willing to wait for him, he'd like to see what they could have together. Would she be willing to wait? Was she even interested?

As soon as he got home from church, he asked his mother if she could watch the twins. He threw together a turkey sandwich and headed out to saddle his favorite mount, a blood-bay mare named Calamity, who'd earned her name with more than one fiasco over the years.

He took off down the trail at a gallop. Riding usually helped him clear his head. He could communicate with horses without the strain of lipreading and guessing at human body language. With people, he was always wondering if his responses were appropriate to what had been said. He always knew if his horses understood him or not.

Today the tension didn't leave him, no matter how hard he rode. Calamity could feel his anxiety and was skittish, throwing her head and bucking when he reined her in.

He ran a gloved hand down her neck. "Easy, girl. It's not your fault I'm antsy today." He dismounted and slid the reins over Calamity's head to lead her on foot.

"Maybe I can walk off some of this pent-up energy instead of making you do all the hard work," he told the horse, who nickered in response. "No sense transferring all my worries to you, right?"

How had his life fallen apart so quickly—

and just when it was starting to make a little sense for once? He could only hope that he was misreading Faith's signals.

But could he really ask her to get in the middle of his mess of a life? She'd already done so much for him. How could he ask her for more?

He wasn't foolish enough to believe he'd seen the last of Susie. She'd get drunk or high and forget what a disaster last night had been, forget that he'd forbidden her to return until she got her life together. She'd pop up whenever and wherever she wanted.

He felt confident he could protect the twins while they were still babies, but what would happen later, when the girls were old enough to interact with her?

How would he be able to protect them then?

The alternative was taking legal measures, but he wasn't sold on that avenue, either, not when there was the possibility of the courts giving Susie custody. They couldn't see what he saw. There was just too much at stake.

His boots were giving him a blister on his ankle. In total opposition to the country song that suggested otherwise, his boots *weren't* meant for walking—at least for the distance he had gone today. He had to be several miles outside Serendipity town limits by now.

He groaned. Walking away from his problems wasn't going to make them go away. He needed to turn around and face them like a man—and in this case, a very special kind of man.

A daddy.

He mounted Calamity and turned her back toward town, letting her pick an easy gait and giving her her head. She knew the way back to the ranch without him directing the way. Slumped in his saddle and lost in thought, he didn't realize where Calamity had taken him until he saw the brand-new sign proudly marking Untamed Mustang Refuge.

Apparently, he'd been unconsciously directing the horse, after all.

He reined in, hesitating. Faith hadn't seemed too keen on seeing him this morning. She hadn't even come over to say hi to him. Of course, he hadn't approached her, either, having felt the unspoken tension between them.

He didn't get it. Last night they'd seemed so close. Now he felt as if there was a chasm between the two of them and neither of them knew how to cross it. *He* certainly didn't have a clue what had changed. The aisle that split the church sanctuary might as well have been the Grand Canyon.

Now that he thought about it, she'd started acting peculiar just after they'd stolen that moment together. She'd been gracious to a fault and genuinely appeared to enjoy interacting with his family. She'd even handled his brothers' teasing remarks about all the forks, giving every bit as good as she got. She'd insisted on helping clean the dishes, even though Alice had protested heartily that she was a guest in the house.

But she'd avoided being alone with him again. He'd had every intention of walking her out to her truck, where he hoped he might steal another kiss, to re-create the emotions he'd felt the first time. He didn't know where it would lead, if anywhere, but for the first time in years he'd seen a glimpse of something positive in his life.

First the twins.

And now Faith—except that she'd skipped out on him when he'd gone to change Violet's wet diaper. He was out of the room for no more than two minutes, but when he returned, Faith was gone. She'd left without giving him as much as a wave goodbye. He thought he deserved that much, at least, for all they'd been through together that evening.

Then again, maybe he was imagining the whole thing and he was the one creating the tension and the chasm. Maybe he was making a big deal out of nothing. He was probably being hypersensitive because seeing Susie again had brought back all of those bad memories.

The physical pain. The horror. The shame.

But that was the past, and the past was over.

Sitting here at the entrance of Faith's ranch wasn't going to do anybody any good, least of all him. He wouldn't know how Faith was feeling until he asked her. He needed to stop hesitating and start acting like a mature man instead of a brainless teenager.

Even though it was a day of rest, Jax knew he wouldn't find Faith in her still practically unlivable house. Ranch work didn't take a Sabbath, and though he'd helped her hire a couple of responsible teenage wranglers to assist her, she wasn't the type of person to delegate everything to someone else.

No—she'd be in the barn or the corral or the meadow, or maybe riding her gelding Alban around her thousand acres checking her fences for breaks. Even if she had nothing pressing to do, she would want to be out with her horses. They were her happy place.

He looped the reins back over Calamity's neck and led her out to the pasture to graze, then turned back toward the barn.

He'd reached the entrance and was waiting for his eyes to adjust to the dim interior when a shadow came whirling like a Tasmanian devil out from around the corner of the door.

Faith was walking backward, hauling heavy buckets of feed and overcompensating on the weight. Before he knew what was happening, her back had collided with his chest.

He reacted instinctively, wrapping his arms around her waist to keep her from falling, but he could do nothing about the buckets of grain she was carrying.

The aluminum buckets clanged to the dirt, and the oat mixture exploded into the air as if it had been set off by a detonator.

Faith shrieked in alarm and turned on him, a hand over her heart and her face flushed pink with exertion.

Or maybe anger.

"*What* do you think you are doing here?" she demanded, glaring up at him. "You nearly scared the life out of me. And just look what you've done to my feed!"

So—it was anger, then.

"I was getting ready to call out for you," he said, grabbing one of the buckets and crouching to scoop the oats back into it. Most of the feed was salvageable, although some of the grain would be lost in the dirt. "I was just letting my eyes adjust to the darkness first."

She harrumphed and grabbed the other bucket, scooping up the nearest pile of grain and tossing it inside.

"I apologize, Faith. Really. Come on. I didn't mean to startle you."

"No biggie." She didn't meet his gaze. Instead, she tossed more oats into her bucket with a little more fervor than was strictly necessary.

Jax sat back on his heels and braced his hands on his thighs. He waited for her to stop her frantic activity, but it was almost as if she didn't see him there.

Except he knew she did.

"Faith," he said, reaching for her elbow. "Will you just stop for a second?"

She brushed her hair out of her eyes with the back of one hand and finally met his gaze. "What?"

"Why are you mad at me?"

She stood and shook her head. "I'm not mad. You startled me. That's all." Her eyes narrowed on him. "Why are you here on a Sunday, anyway?"

Jax sighed inwardly. Stubborn woman. He wasn't talking about their little run-in in the stable just now, and she knew it.

"You were avoiding me in church this morning. Do you want to tell me what is going on with you?"

"No, not really."

She stood and grabbed Jax's bucket from him, striding off to the corral. He followed close behind, jamming his hands into the front pockets of his jeans so he wouldn't give in to the sudden urge to throttle her.

She hung the buckets on a hook in the corral. Two black-and-white pinto yearlings huddled as far away from Faith as possible until she tapped her hand against one of the buckets.

"Come on, guys. This is the good stuff."

She leaned her elbow against the corral fence and waited. Jax thought her posture was a little too stiff and was fairly certain he was the cause of it.

He still had a pretty major learning curve where women were concerned, especially Faith, but he knew enough to know that now might not be the best time to mention anything posture or tension related. He didn't have a death wish.

The colts snuffed and snorted, but eventually the idea of a gourmet meal won out over having to eat it with a strange human standing next to them.

"They're beautiful," he remarked when the horses were well into their dinner.

"Aren't they? It's hard to believe they were considered expendable. Some cattle ranchers didn't want the wild horses grazing on public land near their ranches. Grass guzzlers, they call them. So when new foals are born, it doesn't go over very well with those ranchers. These two sweet colts were in what they call *temporary holding*, although it's rarely temporary. More like a way to thin out the herd."

"They look like they're in pretty good condition." Slowly and smoothly, he moved closer to them to get a better look. One of the horses briefly pinned his ears back, but Jax's presence didn't stop him from eating. What was one more human in the big scheme of things?

"They are. The vet gave them both a clean bill of health. I'm just giving them a little extra nutritional head start. I've been introducing them to the herd a few horses at a time while you were out working with Fuego. They're doing well. Willow seems to have taken a special interest in them. I think they're about ready to be able to taste full freedom, or at least as much as I can offer them."

Faith appeared to have lost the tension in her shoulders. She was breathing easier, and her hazel eyes were gleaming, a beautiful mixture of greens and golds, just as they always were when she talked about her herd.

Horses.

Jax realized with a sudden burst of inspiration that horses were their bridge to communication, the one thing they had absolutely in common. No matter what else was going on between them—and he was still completely in the dark as to what that might be—they had horses.

"Look, I don't want to push you, but—"

"You already did, remember?" she said with a strained laugh. "You nearly knocked me down back there in the barn."

"Hey. You ran into me, remember?" he protested.

"Only because you were looming in the doorway as silent as a mouse."

Jax smiled and relaxed a little. He'd never been compared to a mouse before. A monster, maybe.

Anyway, if Faith was bantering with him, it couldn't be all bad, could it? Did a man have room to hope?

"Can I help you with your chores?" he offered. He figured he might as well stay on neutral ground, at least for the time being. Eventually the serious conversation would have to happen, but it didn't have to be right this second.

She shook her head, and Jax felt her refusal like a punch in the gut. She'd always been happy to have his help before. For her to turn it down now must mean that she had decided to push him away. The kiss last night, and the comfortable companionship they'd built over the preceding weeks—she'd decided she didn't want that. Didn't want *him*.

Her rejection hurt. Really hurt. He never should have let himself become vulnerable to another woman. He shouldn't have allowed her to get close to him. Hadn't he learned anything from Susie?

"Okay, well then, I guess I'll—"

"No—I mean, I've finished with all my chores for now," she qualified.

He let out a breath he hadn't even realized he'd been holding, but it caught tight in his throat, giving it a ragged quality.

"If you want to take Calamity's tack off and give her a quick rubdown in one of the stalls, I'll go up to the house and make us a pot of coffee." She glanced up at the sky to the gray clouds rolling in. "It looks like it might rain."

"A hot cup of coffee would be nice but…" He paused, unsure how he should frame his question without heading down the wrong path again.

"But what?" She tilted her chin and regarded him calmly. There was no anger or frustration in her expression. In fact, Jax couldn't read it at all. He had no idea what she was thinking.

That was unnerving.

He cleared his throat. "I was just wondering—why the sudden change of heart? Last night I thought we were—" He paused to find the right word. "Close. This morning I had the distinct impression you were avoiding me."

She sighed with so much emotion that all he could think of was how much he wanted to wrap her in his arms, tuck her head under his chin and hold her until the world went away.

But he knew better than to try that right now, not when something was so obviously bothering her—something that involved him.

So it was coffee, then. For now.

She still hadn't responded to his question, and he thought perhaps she wasn't going to. She ran a hand across her cheek, leaving a tiny trail of dirt.

Jax's gaze seized on it, and he clenched his fists to keep from following the line with his finger.

Finally, she spoke. "Ignoring this—*prob-*

lem—isn't going to make it go away. We both live in the same town, attend the same church. You're right. We need to talk. Now is as good a time as any."

Problem?

So she thought he was a problem. Well, it wouldn't be the first time. His chest tightened defensively over his heart. The emotional shields dropped into place.

Faith might not care about his outward scars, but it sounded as if she was about to add to his inward ones. Even if she didn't mean to, and even if she didn't understand what she was doing, her words had the ability to pierce him straight through to his heart.

Because there weren't walls high enough or armor strong enough to protect him from Faith. He shouldn't have let himself develop feelings for her, but he had.

He wouldn't survive another broken heart.

Faith scooped four measures of hazelnut-flavored coffee into the coffeemaker basket, added water and pressed the on button. She had about five minutes max to gather her thoughts, to be able to give Jax a coherent explanation for her completely inexplicable behavior.

She knew what Jax had been through, understood that, especially after the kiss they'd shared, the way she was suddenly backing away from him was hurting him.

She would never in a million years have wanted to be someone who could cause Jax pain, but that didn't change the fact that she was in that very place now. She'd let herself grow close to him, had somehow even encouraged him to have feelings for her. She didn't even know exactly how that had happened, but when he'd turned around and planted one on her, there was no doubt that it *had* happened.

She wished she had been transparent about her past from the get-go. Then he'd understand why the recent events had affected her the way they had.

But she hadn't shared her past with him, and now it was too late. There weren't words to make this better, and there were no excuses. *I'm sorry* wouldn't be good enough. She had to get some distance from him, and no matter what she said, how she tried to explain, he would take it as a rejection—not of their relationship, but of *him*, his very essence, of who he was as a person.

Which was the furthest thing from the truth. It was because she cared for Jax and his sweet, darling baby girls that she could not let herself become more involved with him.

More than anything, she wanted to communicate that message to him, but no matter how she phrased it, she was going to come out sounding trite and clichéd.

It's not you, it's me.

The truth. And the ultimate brush-off.

She heard the screen door open and slam shut and then Jax stomping his boots on the welcome mat. He knew there was no need for him to take his boots off in her house. The stained pink carpet was well beyond repair and would have to be replaced—eventually. Sometime down the road, when she finally got around to repairing the house. And who in their right mind had originally chosen to cover their floor in garish pink carpet, anyway?

"Faith?" Jax called.

"In the kitchen."

He appeared in the main doorway before her statement was finished, which meant he'd been standing right there all along. She raised a brow.

"Last time I didn't call your name fast enough," he explained with the familiar half grin that made her heart dance. "So I thought I'd better be extra careful this time around, just in case you were—you know—walking backward carrying a couple of cups of hot coffee or something. Getting doused with oats is one thing. Scalding-hot liquid is quite another."

"Oh, you," she said, swatting his arm.

He laughed and ducked out of her reach.

Then their eyes met, and their amusement flickered to life, turning to something more akin to a warm fire in a hearth on a cold night.

Oh, why did this have to be so difficult? She'd never felt as much at ease with anyone as she did when she was with Jax. She could be herself with him. He understood her, and she believed she understood him, as well. Their friendship was rock solid.

If only it could remain a friendship.

But it couldn't. There was no possible way of it now. The kiss they'd shared the previous evening had taken the strength of their friendship and woven all kinds of new emotions into it, in a way that she knew they could not now unweave. It was the kind of experience she'd always dreamed of and yet never truly imagined existed.

Chemistry? Undeniable. There were stars and fireworks galore. But as deep as that was, their physical attraction to one another only scratched the surface of their interchange. It was like the lyrics to a song. The accompanying emotions were the music, the melody and harmony weaving in and out of her heart.

And ruining everything.

He pulled out a chair for her at the kitchen table and gestured for her to sit.

"Mugs?" he asked.

"Right above the coffeemaker."

"That's a sensible place to keep them."

"You make it sound like *sensible* is unusual for me."

He poured two cups and set one before her and one across the table before seating himself.

"I would never say any such thing. I'd never even think such a thought. Cream or sugar?"

She shook her head. "I take mine black."

"Yeah. Me, too." He cupped both hands around his mug. "I could never figure out why people dump so many extra calories into a perfectly good zero-calorie beverage."

She choked on a sip of coffee. "Right. Because you're so calorie conscious. I guess you have to watch your weight, don't you, to make sure you still look cute in your skinny jeans?"

He barked out a laugh. Jax was a big man, but he didn't have an ounce of fat on him. He was pure, unadulterated muscle from head to toe. And his jeans looked mighty nice on him, even if they weren't of the skinny variety.

"I'll bet you don't even exercise."

His brow rose. "You mean like running? Or going to work out at the gym?"

She shrugged. "Something like that."

"I hate to break it to you, but there's no gym in Serendipity."

"That's a real shame."

"Not really. I wouldn't use it if there was. And running? Forget that noise. You won't see me running unless I'm being chased by a grizzly bear. And it'll have to be a big bear."

She chuckled. "Wow. And here I figured if you ran across a grizzly, you'd stick around and wrestle the thing."

"Only if you were watching." He winked at her. "Would that impress you?"

"Everything you do impresses me."

His gaze widened, then narrowed. He reached across the table and took her hands.

"You say that," he murmured, distracting her by rubbing his thumbs against her palms in small circles. Plus he was using that *voice*, the one that made Faith melt into a puddle of goo.

How fair was that?

"Something has shifted between us since last night," he continued. "I don't have a clue, but I'm pretty sure you know what it is. Tell me what's bothering you."

She dropped her gaze to where her hands lay in his. How could such big hands be so gentle?

"It's because I kissed you, right? It was too soon? If it was, I apologize. I got so caught up in the emotions of the night that I—"

"Don't apologize," she interrupted. "It wasn't the kiss, exactly, or the timing."

"We can take a step back," he continued, his voice low and urgent. "I can go as slow as you need me to, Faith, but you've got to talk to me. Please tell me what you need."

"I need you to leave me alone." She hated the way she'd blurted it out, but if she hadn't, she knew she would have forever lost her courage.

His gaze clouded and he swallowed hard. He let go of her hands and laid his own flat on the table, staring at his fingers as if they would give him the answers he was seeking.

Faith knew there were no answers. Not for this.

She expected him to make a hasty exit, but when he looked up she could see the determination lining his gaze. He wasn't going anywhere. Not without a better explanation, which she didn't know how to give him.

"No." He frowned and shook his head. "I refuse to believe that. Not after last night. What we have here growing between us, it's real. It's good. You know it and I know it. But you're afraid. Why? Is it because of Susie? Because—"

"It's not Susie. It's the babies."

He rocked back in his chair, clearly stunned. "Rose and Violet?"

"I love those two little girls more than you can possibly imagine."

He let out a breath, reminding Faith of a deflating balloon. Relief flooded his expression.

"What did you think I meant?" she asked in alarm. "Surely you couldn't possibly think that I disliked them?"

"Two babies are a truckload of work," he said. "Some women would consider that a lot of baggage."

"Well, I'm not *some women*."

"No. You're not. You're special." Their gazes met and his eyes flamed.

"And so are your children. Don't you ever let anyone tell you those babies are anything other than the biggest blessings in your life. If a woman doesn't get that, she's not worthy of you."

He nodded. "I agree. But you love my babies

and you are definitely a worthy woman and yet you don't want to be with me. Is that right?"

She pinched the bridge of her nose. "I do want to be with you. Very much. That's the problem."

"Because…?" He frowned over the rim of his coffee cup, his dark brow crinkling over his nose.

"Before I came here, I was in a relationship with a man who—" She paused. This was going to sound like a scripted reveal episode on a reality television show, but it was her story and it was her own fault for waiting this long to tell him the truth.

"Keith had a six-year-old son named Trevor. He introduced me to the boy just a few dates into our relationship."

"How long did it last?"

"Two years. I thought I was in love with Keith, although now, looking back at it, I realize I had no idea what true love was about. There were signs from the beginning that it wasn't a healthy relationship.

"To tell you the truth, I think I stayed solely because of Trevor. His life wasn't remotely stable, and he needed an adult he could trust, not to mention a female role model in his life." She sniffled. "And I loved him."

Tears burned in her eyes despite her best effort to keep them at bay.

Jax picked up his chair and brought it around to her side of the table and then pulled her into his arms.

She didn't stop him, even though it was hardly consistent with her intention of backing away from him. If anything, she was getting more and more involved by the second.

"Keith was never responsible as a man or as a father. I knew he was seeing multiple women, and yet I stayed to keep Trevor out of the cross fire.

"Until one day, out of the blue, Keith told me he never wanted to see me again. I don't know why he waited so long, or why he chose right then to kick me out of his life. I only know that he—he told me I was lousy mother material and that he'd never even consider having me raise his son. I knew in my heart that it wasn't true, but his words still stung and it crushed me that I'd never be able to see Trevor again."

She swept in a deep breath and shrugged helplessly. "That's it, in a nutshell—why it's just me and my horses out here on the range."

At least it had been, until she'd gotten all tangled up with Jax. If only she hadn't attended the auction, or if she'd bid on some nice old married rancher with twenty grand-children. Why had she gone and bid on the most appealing man on the block?

Jax's growl surprised her. "Keith is the big-gest fool who ever walked the planet." His voice was thick with emotion. He leaned back and took her face between his palms, gen-tly stroking away her tears with the pads of his thumbs. "Listen to me, and listen to me good. There is no woman I've ever known who more deserves to be a mother. You will definitely be the greatest mom ever. I com-pletely trust my babies with you. One hun-dred percent. Do you hear me? Those girls already understand that you are someone spe-cial in their lives.

"And in my life, too, Faith. I care for you."

She pulled back and crossed her arms as a shiver ran through her. "I know. I believe you. You know as well as I do that I've already de-veloped special feelings for Rose and Violet, and I know they recognize that in me. But I can't risk going through that kind of experi-ence ever again, Jax.

"You already have the power to break my heart. Every day I'm with you I grow closer and more attached to Rose and Violet. If we ever ended our relationship, I'd be ending my relationship with the twins, as well. I can't do that. I just can't. It wouldn't be fair to them, and it would be devastating to me. And before you say it, I don't think I can just be your friend. Not after last night."

She knew she should stand up and move away from him. She needed to put some physical distance between them. She couldn't think straight when she was looking into his warm chocolate eyes.

She knew that in her head, but she couldn't seem to make her limbs cooperate. She did not protest when he leaned in closer, even when he bent his head to brush his lips over hers. She laid her palm flat against his chest, but it was not to push him away.

She wanted to feel his heart beat.

"I understand," he murmured against her ear. "I do. And I don't claim to know what the answer is right now. I only know I can't let you go. We will find a way, Faith. I promise you that. Do you trust me?"

She nodded and laid her ear where her palm had been, listening to the steady, reassuring thump of his heart, breathing in his familiar scent.

She did trust him. He'd won her over the same way he'd done with Fuego. With lots of patience and hard work. She believed him.

She believed *in* him, probably more than he believed in himself.

They were a fine pair, the two of them, each broken in their own way.

"I'm sorry, Jax. This was a bad time for me to wig out on you this way, what with Susie coming by and all. I didn't mean to add to your grief."

He let out a deep breath and combed his fingers through his thick, dark hair. She sat back in her chair and brought her knees up to her chest, then picked up her coffee cup and took a long, satisfying sip of the now-luke-warm liquid. The hint of hazelnut lingered on her tongue.

"I've been thinking about the situation with Susie. I think I may have to take legal action," he said, stroking a hand down the stubble on his jaw. "I don't know how else to keep her away. But honestly, I hate to go that direction unless I have to. I can give the twins every-thing they need without a government doc-ument telling me to. But I don't trust her to keep her distance, just because it's the right thing to do. Getting custody officially will let me protect the twins from her. I'll get a DNA test done to prove my paternity in case my name isn't listed on the birth certificate."

"That's a good idea."

"And I'm going to do everything I can to keep interacting with Susie on my own terms. I hope—I pray—she wises up and gets the help she needs."

Faith put her hand on his. He linked their fingers.

"What happens if she keeps coming back?"

His lips thinned. "That thought occurred to me. I can't let it keep me up nights, or it will make me crazy. I've got too many good things going on in my life right now to let endless negative possibilities put a damper on it. I'll hire the best lawyer on the planet and fight tooth and nail for the twins. I don't know what I would do without my girls."

"I'm sure you will be able to—"

Her sentence was cut off by the eerie sound of a horse's scream.

Chapter Eight

Jax was on his feet in an instant, rushing toward the door. Faith knocked her cup over and righted it again, not bothering to wipe up the black liquid spreading across the table.

Rain was coming down in sheets, and thunder and lightning boomed and crackled. Jax knew the herd would probably be a little skittish because of the storm, but it shouldn't have put them in an all-out frenzy. Something else was wrong. He could feel it in his gut.

Faith grabbed his elbow, and he shot a glance back to her.

"What's happening?" she asked frantically, and he knew it wasn't the first time she'd asked. Stupid hearing loss.

"I don't know." He held out his hand to her. "Come on. Hurry."

Jax couldn't immediately see what was

causing the herd to act up, but clearly some-thing had majorly spooked them. It was only after they'd turned the corner of the barn that Jax realized what was happening.

Fire.

His scar tissue sparked to life with a scorching itch as if the flame was right on top of it, attacking him again.

The memory was as intense as the light-ning above them. It came in short, sharp bursts like photographic images.

He sees the accident take place in front of him as if it plays out in slow motion. He watches the car's taillights gleam as it flies off an embankment. He hears the sickening crunch of the front end plowing headfirst into a tree.

The shrill horn peals and peals. He wants to cover his ears against the sound. It makes his ears hurt.

He reaches for his cell phone and calls 911, giving his location in a shaky voice.

He runs out in the rain, ignoring the down-pour.

The car is on fire. How can it be on fire in the rain? The driver is slumped over the wheel and doesn't appear to be conscious.

He checks the driver's side door. It is

locked. He runs around to try the passenger door. It is also locked.

He wraps his coat around his hand and punches through the passenger side window.

Once. Twice.

The shattered glass mirrors a spider web but does not break through.

Another punch. He's through. He trips the switch, unlocking all the doors.

The woman in the driver's seat is partially conscious after all, but she's nearly unresponsive. There's a kid who looks to be five or six in a booster seat in the back. He reaches for the booster seat first, unbuckling the belt. He carries the little boy, up the ravine, placing him in the safety of the truck until the paramedics arrive to help him.

He slides back down the ravine to rescue the woman. He knows it's not safe to try to move an injured person, but the car is still on fire. Do cars explode in real life like they do in movies?

He doesn't know. Can he wait, not knowing for sure?

The police are almost here. The fire department. Paramedics. They will know what to do.

But the fire.

The fire.

"Ma'am?" he yells. "Can you walk, if I help you?"

She nods and mumbles something in his ear but he can't understand her. Reaching under her shoulder, he supports her while she climbs out of the car. He walks her step by careful step up the embankment.

She's repeating something over and over, but the rain washes the sound away.

"What?" He leans closer.

"My baby. My baby."

A baby. Is there a baby in the car? Or is she talking about the little boy?

He slides down the hill and forces himself into the backseat of the car. The storm is dark. There is no moon. He searches blindly with his hands for another child.

The engine explodes. The car lists and then overturns. Jax is flung forward, rolling over the backseat and into the front. His head strikes something hot. The last thing he remembers before passing out is the searing pain of skin on hot metal.

"Jax!" Faith was pulling on his arm, desperately trying to get his attention. He didn't know how long his shock had lasted. A few moments at least. "Do you see it? The fire?"

He nodded. The grass fire looked to be somewhere around the third meadow, probably caused by lightning. It might be hampered by the rain, but it was a real threat nonetheless. Fires like this could flare out of control within minutes.

And fire was Jax's worst nightmare come to life.

"What should we do?" Faith asked, wringing her hands. "I'll call 911 as soon as I get back in the barn."

"Yes, that should be the first order of business. I think the fire department should be able to take care of this grass fire fairly easily, but fire is a tricky thing. It's unreliable and has a mind of its own."

Unconsciously, he ran a finger across the scar on his face.

"Oh, Jax." She laid her hand on his scarred cheek and then hugged him fiercely.

"I'm fine. Look, we've got the rain in our favor. I'll get the Bobcat going. I don't know how much trenching I'll be able to do but every little bit helps, to keep the fire from crossing the line and destroying more of your land. And if you can find me a shovel, that will help, too."

"Should I go with you?"

"No. You need to look after the horses. Take Alban and see if you can find the herd and drive them into the corral. They'll be frightened so they may be more difficult than usual, but I know you can do it. It's time to prove your skills, Faith. The horses are going to be pretty stressed. Do whatever you can to keep them calm so you can get them where it's safe."

Faith stepped inside the barn and pulled out her phone, speaking with a 911 operator at the same time she retrieved a shovel for Jax.

He had the Bobcat running by the time she returned. He couldn't tell whether the moisture on her face was from the rain or from tears. He wiped her cheeks with his palms and kissed her forehead.

"Your horses will be fine, Faith. And don't worry. I'll save as much of your property as I can."

She squeezed him so hard he lost his breath.

"I don't care about my stupid land," she said with a sob. "Promise me you'll stay safe. Promise me, Jax."

He framed her face with his hands. "We'll get through this, Faith. Together. God didn't bring us this far to leave us hanging now."

She nodded and set her jaw in determination. "Go."

He hopped into the Bobcat and made it about five feet before he stopped the vehicle again. He strode back to where Faith was still standing and kissed her long and hard.

"I love you."

She placed a palm on his cheek. "Go."

This time he continued down the road on the Bobcat, wishing the vehicle went faster. His good ear strained to hear anything above the roll of the storm and the hum of the engine, trying to make out the sound of stray horses or the sirens of rescue vehicles.

But all he could hear was his own ragged breathing cutting up the night air, growing shorter and more rapid as he drove closer and closer to the one fear he could never quite overcome.

He might not be able to do much to save the land, but he refused to quit now. He would fight with everything in him and do whatever he could. Faith had worked too hard to lose it all now.

And he wasn't going to allow himself to think about what would happen afterward.

He had declared his love for her, which had surprised him as much as it must have done her. She hadn't said she loved him back. He refused to be crushed by that knowledge. She had good reason to guard her heart. He hadn't yet offered her anything permanent and stable that she could trust, that she knew she would be able to depend on forever.

But he would—even if he had to walk through fire to do it.

Faith spent more time than she should have watching Jax leave, bobbing down the road in the little tractor. *Courageous* didn't even begin to describe his efforts, heading off to face his worst fears straight on.

She didn't have that strength. She had waited until Jax was back in the Bobcat before she'd whispered her own vow—

"I love you, too."

There was no way he could have heard it, and that was for the best.

She shook her head to regain her focus and ran back into the barn to grab her horse. She didn't bother tacking Alban up. She bridled him as fast as she could and mounted bareback. It would be a slick, dangerous ride in the pouring rain, especially in the dark, but she had to make sure her horses were safe and there was no time to spare.

She clicked her tongue and urged Alban into a gallop as soon as she had passed through the corral gate. She wished she'd thought to bring a flashlight, but she wouldn't have wanted to take the time to run back to the house to try to find one. She wasn't even sure she owned a flashlight.

Yet another mark on her record. Her learning curve was atrocious.

The storm clouds covered whatever moon there might have been, but the sky lit up with lightning often enough for her to find her way. She knew her property like the back of her hand, so even in the dark she felt confident in her direction.

Hearing the frightened nicker of a horse nearby, she pulled up, trotting toward the east fence where she thought she'd heard the sound.

She suspected it would take her a long time to round up all the horses, especially if they'd spooked and scattered. She prayed none of them had been caught up by the fire.

And she especially prayed for Jax, who had put himself directly in the path of those dreadful flames, just to help her. The physical part of it was bad enough without considering the fight of his life he was probably battling inside his head.

She'd seen his expression when he'd first caught sight of the fire, and she'd recognized the way his gaze faded into the past.

She'd lost him for a good minute as he'd probably relived the horrors of his accident.

And now he was facing a fire again. A different sort of fire, and hopefully not one that would put him in personal danger, but as he'd said, flames were unpredictable and could take on a life of their own.

What if Jax got caught up out there?

If something happened to him, she would never forgive herself. He already had enough scars—inside and out—to last him a lifetime.

He had to stay safe. He'd told her he loved her, and she knew he didn't take those words lightly. It was hard for her to believe she'd even heard him right.

But she couldn't afford to think about that at the moment. His declaration had caught her completely off guard, and it had probably surprised him, as well. It would take her whole mind, body, soul and spirit to work through all the implications.

Right now she needed to keep her head in the game. She had to save her horses and hopefully most of her land.

The sky lit up, and she saw a flash of silver moving in the distance near the east fence in the second meadow, right near where she'd thought she'd heard the sound of horses. The area was about as far away from the fire as the horses could get without access to the corral.

Fuego.

She nudged Alban forward, happy to see her herd's stallion safely out of the way of the fire, even if she wasn't entirely certain he would take her direction to get back to the corral. She wasn't sure she possessed that skill level yet.

But she was all Fuego had, and she would have to be enough.

As she drew nearer she realized it wasn't just Fuego but her entire herd huddled together, with nearly every last horse present and accounted for.

Thank You, Lord.

Performing a quick head count, she realized there was only one horse missing, and she wasn't immediately sure which one. She wouldn't have time to do a full equine roll call until she had them all locked safe in the corral.

Fuego was running around the outside perimeter of the herd, neighing and snorting and keeping his mares and foals all together.

"Well done, Fuego," she said, although she wasn't sure he could hear her voice over the sound of the wind and rain.

Now was the hard part—communicating to the wild horses that they needed to be moved to the corral for their own safety until the fire was extinguished and they could return to the land.

If Fuego bucked her authority, the others would most certainly follow his lead.

She gritted her teeth. If that was the case, then she couldn't let him challenge her.

She adjusted her reins and pulled up beside Fuego, holding out her free hand for him to sniff. She could see the whites of his eyes and realized how close he was to spooking. His grunting was just short of frantic.

She held her breath and ran her palm down his neck. "It's okay, boy. We've got this all under control. You and I have to get your mares and foals to safety. You know that, right, Fuego? This is your band. It's up to you."

She didn't possess Jax's lyrical voice, but Fuego pricked his ears and tossed his head, making snorting noises that almost sounded like speech.

"All right, then. Let's go." She rode to the back of the herd and waved her hands in large back-and-forth motions. "Let's go. Let's go now."

She weaved Alban back and forth a few times and managed to get the herd trotting in the right direction. Fuego seemed to be leading, although he occasionally swung around to urge a straggling colt or mare along.

They made surprisingly good progress, and it wasn't long before they crossed into the first meadow. Now was the hard part. The corral gate didn't have a big enough opening to accept all the horses at once, and she didn't have any help to keep them in any sort of line. She'd have to herd in a few at a time and hope the others didn't wander away.

But it turned out she *did* have help, after all. As she worked, Fuego watched over the rest of his band, keeping them together in a loose circle. It was almost as if he understood what she was doing and he was working with her.

It took her a few minutes, but she was finally ready for the last three horses—Willow and Pilgrim, the first two horses she'd received at Untamed, and Fuego himself.

But when she turned to herd them through the gate, only Willow and Pilgrim remained.

Fuego was gone.

Chapter Nine

Jax stood with his back against the Bobcat and watched the Serendipity Fire Department put out the last of the flames. Though he was standing in the rain, sweat drenched his forehead and salt stung his eyes. The sun was just starting to peek over the horizon, making the smoke look like a misty haze instead of the deadly threat it had felt like last night.

He'd used the small tractor to create as long of a trench as he could and as fast as possible to keep the fire from spreading. He had continued to help once the fire department arrived, but by the end of the night he could see what little good it had done. Despite his best efforts, Faith had still lost close to a hundred acres of grazing turf to the fire. It made him sick to think about.

Chief Jenkins, the fire chief, assured him

that if it hadn't been for his efforts, the damage might have been a whole lot worse.

Jax wasn't satisfied with that answer. The damage was bad enough, and it would set Faith back substantially. If he'd been able to move faster, or if he had carved his trenches closer to the base of the fire…

"I'm going to drive the Bobcat back and check on Faith and the herd," he told Chief Jenkins, who shook his hand.

"You did well, Jax. We appreciate your efforts. The department will finish up things here, and then I'll come up to the house and let Faith know how things stand."

"Thanks for all you've done. I know Faith will want to express her gratitude, as well."

The Bobcat moved at a snail's pace, unlike the previous evening when it seemed to carry him to the fire much faster than he could handle. His heart had been beating out of his chest last night, trying to get to the fire and stop it from attacking Faith's property even as every instinct in his body told him to get as far away from the flames as he could. Now his heart was aching even worse, knowing he had to tell her the bad news about the destruction of her land before Captain Jenkins beat him to it. Better that the information come from a friend than from the fire chief.

He wondered not for the first time how Faith was handling dealing with the herd. He had every belief in her abilities. He just hoped she was aware of how good she was.

He hadn't seen her since they'd split the evening previous, nor had he spotted any stray horses lingering around, so he hoped all had gone well in that regard.

At least God had seen fit to save the house. And hopefully all the horses.

And most important of all, Faith herself.

He'd meant what he'd whispered into her ear the night before. It wasn't some kind of disaster declaration, made only because of adrenaline and the drama of the moment.

He was in love with her. It had started the moment she bid on him at the auction, even if it had only been because she felt a backward sense of compassion for his sorry mug. She'd been by his side through every catastrophe since then—one after another—and they'd had a few beautiful moments, too, such as the times they'd spent together with the twins and the incredible kiss they'd shared.

He'd grown used to having her in his life, helping her with her burdens and letting her help with his, being by her side, enjoying the way she offered up her own brand of strength and compassion, whether he asked for it or not. She was always there for him, no matter what.

And he wanted to be there for her, to protect her, provide for her and love her with his whole heart. If she'd let him, he wanted to take the savings he'd earned over the years as a horse trainer and partner with her to make Untamed everything she imagined it could be, and then some. If it was in his power, he wanted to make her dreams come true.

He also wanted to give her a family no one could take away from her—the family she'd always dreamed of. Wanted to fully entrust to her the care and love of Violet and Rose, giving her the opportunity to open her heart up to the children she'd longed for, completely without fear. He wouldn't be opposed to hearing the pitter-patter of even more little feet somewhere in the future, babies with Faith's hazel eyes and sweet smile.

He wanted to give her the world.

But was she willing to accept it from him? Did fear have too strong a hold on her heart for her to consider opening it to him? She didn't seem to want to fall in love again—and who was he to change her mind? A battered, scarred wreck of a man. But a man who loved her with all his heart. Would that be enough?

With nowhere else to turn, Jax decided to

hand the situation over to God. When he'd become a father, it had given him a whole new outlook as to who God was as a Father, and Jax found himself turning to the Lord more often for help and guidance.

He prayed now as he drove, asking God for all the right words to express the feelings in his heart. All of this meant nothing if he couldn't convince her she could trust him with her heart, if she couldn't finally lay her past to rest and realize she could truly hope for the future with him and the twins.

He of all people knew how hard it was to keep the past in the past, especially since *his* past seemed to keep popping back up in his life. But he also knew he couldn't let fear keep him from living his life to the fullest.

Last night Faith hadn't shared his sentiment, or at least she hadn't said the words aloud. It was his own fault that he'd picked the least opportune moment possible to make such a declaration.

His hopes were sky-high as he approached the ranch house, but he also felt as vulnerable as he'd ever been in his entire life. Faith was a kind woman, but even a compassionate rejection might be more than he could handle right now.

He was tired of hiding from life for fear of

rejection. And Faith held that in the palm of her hand. If she didn't love him, then so be it. He would have to try to find satisfaction in being her friend. And he would keep trying to earn her trust and respect.

Just as long as she stayed in his life.

He spotted her long before she saw him. She was leaning against the corral fence, speaking to the horses. Alban's back was bare and his reins loosely tied to the fence.

At first glance it looked as if she'd managed to round up the entire herd. He was impressed with her skills, but then, he'd known she could do it. Even in the dark, and even in the pouring rain. When she set her mind on something, she accomplished it.

Just look how fast she'd learned how to handle running the ranch. For someone who'd not grown up with horses, she displayed considerable finesse with them. She had adapted far more gracefully than he had taken to caring for his twins. He still felt awkward sometimes when he was faced with daddy duties.

As soon as she saw him unfold himself from the Bobcat, she jumped down off the fence and ran to him, throwing her arms around his neck and squeezing him so hard she was choking him. He laughed and grabbed her waist, whirling her around and around.

He was so happy it took him a second to figure out she wasn't laughing with him. She was shaking so hard her teeth were chattering.

He pulled back to look at her face. He was surprised to see tears pouring down her cheeks. His gaze met hers.

"Sweetheart, what's wrong? Are you hurt?"

"I'm just so happy to see you."

"Well, that's good to know." He grinned and shook his head. He'd never understand why women cried when they were happy.

She touched his shoulder, his face, his ear, gently running her fingers against his scars. In some ways it was the same thing Susie had done, but it was such a different kind of caress that it was like night and day. There wasn't disgust or pity in her fingertips, nor even kindness or compassion. It was as if she was reassuring herself of his reality by touching those marks that were uniquely his to bear.

She sighed and brushed her palm down his whiskered cheek. He laid his hand over hers, holding her to him. "The fire is out, Faith. It's over."

He was about to tell her about the damage to her property, but she spoke first.

"I lost him."

What? Lost who? Had one of the horses perished in the fire?

"I'm sorry, Jax. I don't know what happened."

"To...?"

"Fuego. And after all you did for him. It was the weirdest thing I've ever experienced. And then to have it end like this—it just hurts my heart."

She took Jax's hand and threaded her fingers through his, drawing him toward the corral.

"By the time I found the horses, Fuego had rounded up practically the whole herd and had driven them to the eastern part of the second meadow."

"About as far away from the fire as he could get. That's my smart boy."

"I was shocked. He seemed to know what he needed to do to preserve the band."

"As I'm sure you're learning, horses are intelligent."

"I've always known that."

He smiled down at her. Maybe not always, but she certainly knew now.

"I herded the mares and foals back to the corral just like you told me to do. Fuego helped me, nudging the foals along and rounding up the occasional straggler."

She groaned in dismay. "I got them as far as the corral without any problems. I knew I was one horse short when I did a head count in the field. I couldn't take the time to figure which horse I was missing until I got them all rounded up in the corral. It broke my heart to even think about leaving a horse out there on its own, but I knew I had to put the well-being of the band over that of the one horse.

"The corral gate isn't big enough for me to be able to herd all the horses at once, so I rounded up three at a time. Fuego kept the rest of the band together while I did the herding. It was as if we were working as a team."

He nodded. "You were."

Her smile was tired, and though her tears had slowed, they hadn't stopped.

"Near the end I had three horses left—Willow, Pilgrim and Fuego. But when I got ready to herd them in, I discovered Fuego had disappeared. I looked around and he was just—*gone.*"

"Hmm. That's odd."

"The horses in the corral were spooking all over the place. My presence seemed to calm them. I just couldn't justify leaving an entire herd of frightened wild horses cooped up in a corral by themselves to look for Fuego, even though I knew that's where they'd be safest."

"So you stayed with them," he guessed. "It was the right thing to do."

"But Fuego—"

"Is probably fine," Jax finished for her. "You said it yourself. He's a smart horse. He managed to get all the rest of the herd away from the fire. I doubt he'd go charging into it himself."

"I just keep thinking about how he got caught up in the lumber. If anything else happened to him, I'm not sure my heart would be able to stand it."

"I'll go look for him," he assured her. "Or better yet, we can go together. The horses will be fine unsupervised for an hour now that the fire is out and the sun is up. We'll put them in the first meadow and they can graze. Did you ever determine who else was missing?"

"A pregnant mare. Prada. She's close to her time. I'm praying nothing bad happened to her."

"We'll look for her, as well." He ran his gaze over her mount. "Please don't tell me you rode Alban bareback last night." He knew he sounded like a badgering schoolteacher, but he was soaked and exhausted beyond belief from staying up all night, and the thought of Faith galloping around bareback in the dark with slick rain pelting her and her wet mount was more than he could handle.

Didn't she know she could have hurt herself, fallen off and hit her head on a rock? His chest tightened at the thought.

She frowned. "I didn't want to take the time to tack up. As far as I was concerned, every second counted, and I still stand by that decision."

"Except that a horse's bare back is especially slippery when it's wet, and it would have taken all of five minutes to put a saddle on him. What would have happened if you'd hurt yourself?" His voice rose. "Did it even occur to you that you might be putting yourself in danger?"

She scoffed. "Of course it did. And I didn't have a lot of time to think through all of the implications. But now that I'm looking back on it, I would do exactly the same thing again, so stop bugging me about it."

Jax growled in frustration. Stubborn woman.

"Well, we're saddling him this time. Did you get your second riding horse in, or are we doubling up on Alban?"

"*Thankfully*," she said, emphasizing the word, "he showed up the day before yesterday. He's a beautiful quarter horse named Brobie. I'm warning you—he's only green broke. I'm not sure he's ready to ride in the open country yet."

Jax didn't care one whit if the horse was green broke or purple broke or if he had ever seen a saddle at all. Grumbling under his breath, he tacked up both horses. The woman was riding with a saddle this time.

He mounted Brobie and waited for her to mount Alban. "We should check the east fence where you found Fuego and the herd last night," he decided, knowing he sounded like a dictator but unable to temper his tone.

She lifted her chin and glared at him. "I agree."

Hmmph. Well, at least they agreed on something.

He led them at an easy lope, just fast enough that talking was difficult. He should probably be telling her all he knew about the fire and the damage to her land, but that news wasn't going anywhere. He'd let her regroup from one crisis at a time.

And try, this time, not to be so grumpy about it. He owed her an apology for being so short with her. She was still new to ranches and horses. So she'd made a mistake. Nothing bad had come of it. She was fine. *He'd* been the one to make a big deal about it.

He scowled, angry at himself. After today,

with his huge display of bad temper, it would be a wonder if she agreed to marry him.

Marry him?

Yes. That's what he'd been dancing around when he'd been thinking of babies and families and offering Faith security and safety. He just hadn't formulated it in words, so much.

Now that he had the idea in his head, though, he liked it. What said *forever* like a diamond engagement ring?

Aaaand now he was starting to sound like a jewelry shop commercial. He wanted to provide a permanent commitment and express his love, but he hoped he wouldn't get as sappy as all that.

Was he getting ahead of himself? Probably. Just the previous night, he'd told her he loved her—and had then walked off without giving her a chance to respond. Maybe she was just waiting for the crisis to pass before letting him down gently. He knew with a bone-deep certainty that he wanted to spend the rest of his life with her. On the other hand, he had no idea what she wanted.

He just hoped it was him.

And he also hoped that she wouldn't stay mad at him after their little spat this morning. He was glad to know she wasn't the kind of woman who held grudges.

But he wasn't about to propose out in a field on horseback while they were missing horses and they were both soaked to the bone and she was still mad at him for something stupid he'd said. He'd wait until today's chaos was in the past, and then he'd tell her everything—how much he loved her, how he wanted to build a life with her, how beautifully he thought their hopes and dreams for the future could mesh together. And then he'd ask her to marry him.

But none of that was going to happen today.

Faith surged ahead of him and cantered to the fence line, riding a few hundred yards before pulling up and returning to his side. He was struggling with the green-broke colt, who wanted to bolt instead of stand still.

"This is where they were last night, but I don't see any sign of Fuego or the mare."

"Then we've got to keep riding." Rats. He sounded like a dictator again.

Way to go, King Jax.

Thankfully, Faith didn't recognize his tone, or else she chose to ignore it.

Faith's land was fairly flat with only minor hills and ridges and a few random trees in the whole thousand acres. The horses had to be somewhere out of sight. He refused to think of any other outcome for them. Not until he had to.

"What about the copse of trees over by the stream?" she suggested. "I know some of the mares and foals like to hang out there."

That area was fairly close to where the fire had been. Too close, by Jax's estimation. Fuego wouldn't have gone that near to the flames. Unfortunately, it was more likely that he'd found a break in the fence and was long gone by now.

And the pregnant mare? She was anybody's guess. A crazed mare about to foal might have run straight into the fire.

Jax didn't want to suggest either of these possibilities. Not yet. But he didn't have any better alternatives to offer her, so he agreed with her suggestion and trailed her to the water. They followed along the streambed for about fifteen minutes before they heard distressed whinnying coming from the very copse of trees where Faith had guessed she would be.

Prada was lying on her side, her body covered with sweat. Her skin shook and she grunted and snorted and threw her head, clearly straining with the effort of pushing out the foal. Jax didn't know how long she'd been there, but it appeared a new life was about to make its entrance into the big wide world.

With a little cry of distress, Faith slid out of the saddle and ran toward the mare.

Jax wanted to call out to her, but before he had a chance, Fuego came out of nowhere, neighing and bucking angrily. The stallion had appointed himself protector of the laboring mare, and he wasn't happy about humans coming anywhere near her.

Jax knew his green-broke horse would be useless in this situation, and he had only seconds to spare before the stallion charged Faith.

He threw himself off the colt as if he were bulldogging, landing halfway across Fuego's back. He grabbed a handful of mane and struggled to pull himself onto the horse's back. Fuego turned his head and snorted, then threw his weight to one side and then the other, rearing to the front and then the back, turning in tight circles and trying desperately to dislodge his unwelcome rider.

"Easy, boy," he called, but the horse was too wound up to listen to his voice.

Jax somehow managed to stay on Fuego's back. He'd never had any inclination to try to ride a wild mustang stallion, bareback or otherwise, and he didn't want to now, but when the alternative was seeing Faith plowed down by an overprotective band leader, he'd do whatever he had to do. He wanted to yell at Faith to get away from the mare, to go back to Alban where she'd be safer, but Fuego's bucking kept jolting the breath out of him before he could speak.

Faith was hunched over by the mare's side, stroking her neck and speaking to her in soft tones. She seemed entirely unaware of the explosion of silver stallion going on behind her. The stream was rushing loudly beside them, swollen from the previous night's storm. The sound of the frothing water, on top of the mare's pained grunts, must have been enough to block out the noise of Fuego's temper tantrum.

"Faith!"

She turned in his direction and her eyes widened, her mouth gaping in fright.

Jax could feel his grip on Fuego faltering and knew he wouldn't be able to keep the stallion away from the mare—and Faith—for much longer. He opened his mouth one more time to try to warn her, but his words were lost at the same time he lost his seat.

He landed hard on his bad shoulder, and the pain of his scar roared to life, but he ignored it, pushing himself to his feet and running full force toward Faith.

He couldn't see Fuego but knew the stallion must be right behind him. Faith's eyes were still glued to his.

He charged forward and scooped her up by the waist. She screamed in alarm. He twisted hard, just barely missing the angry muzzle of the charging horse.

"Run," he said, pushing her in the direction from which they'd come. "Run and don't look back."

She cast a look over her shoulder and apparently saw Fuego and realized what danger she was in, because she actually listened to him. She tucked her head and ran, following the path of the streambed.

Jax turned back to the stallion, who was stomping and snorting, the whites of his eyes a reflection of his defensive frame of mind.

Jax slowly raised his hands. "Easy there, boy. Faith didn't mean to interrupt. She just wanted to see how Prada was doing. No harm, no foul."

Fuego snorted again but didn't charge him.

Progress. Jax let out his breath and calmed his posture. Fuego would sense any stress or tension Jax carried in his body. They'd already had quite a run-in today. He knew he probably wasn't on top of the stallion's friends list right now.

He backed up until he was even with Alban. If he could somehow manage to get mounted, he'd hopefully be able to handle Fuego and watch the mare for signs of distress, but it was a risk. Fuego could very easily charge him and prevent him from ever mounting Alban.

"It's okay, boy. Remember, we're the good guys," he said, keeping his voice low and even as he hooked his hand over the saddle horn and put his foot into the stirrup. "We're glad to see you both are safe, you know. The three of you, I mean. And I totally get why you'd want to keep an eye on one of your mares. You're a good boy."

Jax swung his leg over Alban's body and shifted his weight in the saddle.

Fuego hadn't moved but was still eyeing him warily.

"Let's just make sure everything is well with the foal, and then I'm out of here," he promised, carefully watching Fuego's body language for any sign of a sudden movement.

He glanced behind him, but Faith was out of sight. He hoped she'd keep on running and wouldn't get it in her head to turn back over a mistaken sense of obligation toward him or the horses.

He watched the mare for a few more minutes until two wet legs appeared. Good. It looked as if the foal was in the right position for an easy birth. It would have been even easier for Prada if he was able to get down and offer her a bit of assistance, but there was no way he was going to put Fuego to the test again. That was a battle he knew he would lose, and he respected the stallion for that.

"Come on, girl," he cheered quietly. "You can do it."

The mare snorted, and with another big push the foal emerged and immediately started wriggling around. Prada whickered and rolled to her feet, nudging for her little chestnut foal to do the same.

Jax chuckled as the wobbly-legged foal struggled to follow its mama's lead. Fuego snorted and trotted back and forth around the area, acting like a proud papa even though it wasn't his foal.

I know how you feel, buddy. I've got a couple of kids myself. And even though I didn't know them before they were born, I couldn't be prouder of them.

Jax watched Fuego for a few more minutes and observed the mare and foal. He probably wouldn't have kept a stallion in the same meadow with a mare about to foal, but in this case it had turned out fine. Better than fine. All three horses were thriving.

And his job was done, at least for the time being. He had to find Faith before she managed to jog all the way back up to the house by herself. He nudged Alban's side and reached for Brobie's lead, frankly impressed that the green-broke colt hadn't bolted off somewhere during all the chaos. He'd be a good horse and a fine addition to Faith's stable. It would be nice for her to have more than one riding horse, if nothing else than for emergencies such as this one.

He leaned forward and all out galloped, enjoying the wind in his face, which, now that he thought about it, must look smeared and sticky from smoke and sweat. It was a wonder Faith hadn't said anything about it. She'd looked at him as if he was the most handsome man she'd ever seen.

So he was deaf and she was blind.

He caught up with her less than half a mile from the house. She wasn't running, but she was...*striding*. Stomping, maybe, her arms flinging back and forth as if she were punching the air.

He reined in beside her and dismounted, pulling the reins over Alban's head and handing them to her. She took them without slow-ing her pace or speaking to him. She hadn't even glanced at him since he'd ridden up.

So she was still mad at him, then.

He supposed he deserved it. And she might very well have misinterpreted his earlier actions with Fuego. She'd been concentrating on the mare. She probably hadn't seen him wrestling with the stallion or realized the possibility of her getting trampled under Fuego's mighty hooves.

And then there was the issue of him scooping her up like a cowboy loading a sack of oats in the back of his pickup truck. He'd tossed her around with just about as much finesse.

She whirled on him and pounded her fists into his chest. "What in the world were you thinking?"

Jax opened his mouth, probably to try to explain his side of things, but Faith was too angry to let him get a word in edgewise.

"You could have been killed, you crazy cowboy. And it would have been all. My. Fault! I can't believe I did something so stupid."

"It wasn't stupid. You were only thinking about the welfare of your mare."

"Right. And not that Fuego wouldn't be

happy about me messing with one of his mares. Or that you would jump in to save me, putting yourself at risk, like you always do."

He had put his arms around her waist, and now he tightened his grip on her, tilting his head so his gaze caught hers.

"Did you even know Fuego was there?"

"Well, no. But that's beside the point. I put you in mortal danger."

He laughed.

Laughed!

Faith found nothing funny about this situation. She'd almost lost the love of her life before she'd even gotten to tell him he was the love of her life.

"I have to admit I never wanted to be a bronc rider. Now I'm certain I don't ever want to rodeo. I'll leave that kind of craziness to my ex-bull-riding brother."

"I can't believe you actually got on Fuego's back," she breathed. It was totally wrong in a million different ways, and she'd been scared out of her mind, but she had to admit it had been magnificent to watch—now that it was over and Jax was safe in her arms.

"And stayed there." He puffed out his chest and flexed his biceps. "For a minute, anyway."

"Yeah. Long enough for me to realize what

a terrible mistake I had made. He didn't hurt you, did he? After I took off running? I know you took quite a sharp fall. You don't have any new bites for me to bandage?"

He kissed her forehead. "Other than a couple of bumps and bruises, I came out unscathed. Alban helped me out when I needed him."

"He's a good horse."

"So is Fuego."

"I know. He was just being a wild stallion, right?"

"The best kind."

"How is Prada? She looked pretty awful when I was there with her."

"That's because she was just about to give birth. She's fine now, and you have a new little sweet chestnut filly in your herd."

"Oh, Jax." She tightened her arms around him. "I thought maybe there was something wrong with Prada. Or the baby. And I was so afraid Fuego was going to go ballistic on you." She shuddered and tears poured from her eyes.

She dashed them away with the back of her hand.

"I never cry when I'm frightened," she said. "Although admittedly I've never been *this* frightened before. Lately it seems I cry at the drop of a hat, but usually I only bawl when I'm angry about something."

He nodded solemnly. "Good to know. So if I see you crying, I should turn and walk the other direction."

She swatted his shoulder. "Stop giving me a hard time. I was really scared for you."

"Hey, who would tease you if I wasn't around to do it?"

"Exactly my point."

"Then I guess I'd better stay."

"In one piece, thank you."

"If you insist." He lowered his head and brushed his lips across hers. "We need to talk."

"Didn't we start last night with this same conversation?"

His eyes widened. "I hope not. I thought you were going to dump me."

"I was."

"Then I guess it's a good thing that the fire interrupted us." Jax paused and lifted his head. "Whoops. I forgot you have company."

"Company?"

"Chief Jenkins. He said he was going to come up to the house after the fire department was finished on your land. He wants to give you a report of the damage. It's not as bad as it could have been, but—"

"Jax. I can't believe you didn't mention this earlier. Here we are meandering along, and the fire chief is probably sitting on my front porch. What am I going to do? I can't invite him inside. My house is…"

"Unlivable?" he supplied for her.

"I was going to say *messy*, but I guess *un-livable* is another way to put it." She tossed the reins over Alban's neck. "I've really got to go if he's waiting."

Jax sighed heavily and shrugged his shoulders as if he was carrying a great weight upon them. "Every time I think we have a minute to finally talk, something happens."

"I know." She blew him a kiss. "Tomorrow. I promise."

They had a lot to talk about, but it was only after she'd ridden away that she realized she hadn't told Jax the one thing that really mattered most.

She hadn't said *I love you*.

She hadn't said *I love you*.

Jax had hoped he might hear those words from her lips, especially after he'd bull-dogged-slash-bronc ridden a wild stallion on her behalf.

She'd been grateful enough, and her kiss had been both sweet and thorough. Sweet and thorough enough to banish nearly all of his doubts about her loving him back, after all.

But she hadn't said the words.

So did he wait until he was sure about her feelings before he proposed?

He didn't want to wait. He wanted to get back up on that stupid makeshift auction block in front of the entire blinking town and announce over the loudspeaker that he'd fallen in love with one very pretty mustang rescuer.

But that was out, so he had to come up with something a little cleverer to surprise his hopefully soon-to-be bride. Something that he could share with the whole world and yet would be personal, just for her.

He had the perfect plan in mind, but it was going to take some juggling on his part to pull it all together. He started by talking to his mom, his brothers and Laney, who all agreed they couldn't think of a better way for him to pop the question.

From there it was just a matter of spreading the word to everyone in Serendipity that Faith needed a bit of assistance around her ranch. It was actually Jax who needed the real help, but he couldn't carry out his plans without the town's full support.

Everyone had heard of the grass fire, so it

was no great stretch to visit Cup O' Jo's and plant the seed in Jo's ear that Faith's house could really use an overhaul. And telling Jo was just about the same thing as telling the whole town. That woman could spread the word like nobody's business. He arranged for everyone to meet at Faith's ranch on Saturday, and on the off chance Faith visited town, asked his neighbors and friends to be hush-hush about it.

He wanted this to be the surprise of a lifetime.

He spent the week making lists and ordering materials. He even made a special trip into San Antonio for a ring. He still preferred to shop in Serendipity over a larger city, but a man had to make an exception once in a while, such as for the woman he loved.

He called Faith on Thursday evening to set the stage for the Saturday event. He wanted it to be a surprise, but he didn't want to accidentally catch her airing her literal laundry or anything embarrassing like that.

He intended to tell her that he and the vet would be coming by to check up on the new filly, but when Faith answered the phone, he didn't get past hello.

"Where have you been? I thought maybe

Fuego caught up with you and stampeded you, after all."

"What?"

"You were the one who said we needed to talk. Wasn't that supposed to happen Monday?"

Jax frowned. His brain wasn't catching up as fast as Faith was speaking. He was feeling all happy and giddy and barely able to contain himself from belting out his love for her, and she was mad at him?

"I—er—"

"You can say anything, Jax. That you got busy at the ranch. That the twins caught pinkeye. Just please give me one good reason why you've left me hanging for nearly a week, or I'll hang up this phone right now."

Because I've got a ring in my pocket?

No. He couldn't tell her that. He *wanted* to tell her that, but it would ruin the surprise.

"I was busy. I *am* busy with something important that just couldn't wait. I've got some—*construction* issues I've been dealing with. Nothing I'd want to bother you with."

Until Saturday.

Her silence was deafening. It was worse than her expressing her hurt feelings.

"Look, I didn't mean to neglect you. I forgot we even had something going on Monday."

"Every week, Jax. Every single week you are over here all the time, helping out with the horses or fixing my fences or *something*. And then suddenly, this week of all weeks, when we're supposed to sit down and have a serious discussion, you are gone, like you dropped off the face of the planet. What am I supposed to think?"

He didn't know how to answer that question.

"You could have called me."

"I shouldn't have had to."

He sighed. "You're right. I should have called. But I'm not avoiding you." He kind of was, but not for the reasons she thought. "I'll make it up to you, I promise."

"Really?"

"Yes, really. Or don't you trust me?"

She mumbled something under her breath.

"What was that?"

"Yes, Jax, I trust you. I'm asking myself why at this point, but I trust you."

"Good. I'm glad to hear it."

"So are we ever going to have that talk, or have you moved on to bigger and better things?"

He started to laugh and then quickly smothered it.

Bigger and better things. Definitely.

"I called because I wanted to bring the vet out to see the little chestnut filly of Prada's. You know, just to make sure she's faring well?"

"I've been keeping an eye on her. She's nursing well and Prada is a good mother. But I won't say no to the vet taking a look at her."

Whew. His ruse was going to stand, then. For a second there he'd been worried. He hadn't thought about what he was going to do if she'd said no.

"Okay, I'll see you Saturday morning. Say about seven o'clock? We can talk afterward if you'd like."

"Sure. And Jax?"

"Hmm?"

"If you don't mind, will you bring the babies? I miss them almost as much as I miss you."

"Sure. I can bring the babies."

And my family, and everyone else in town. Jax hung up smiling.

Chapter Ten

Faith was dressed and ready at five thirty in the morning on Saturday. She'd put on a new blouse and had spent extra time on her hair.

To meet with the vet. Jax was going to razz her for sure, even if he knew perfectly well that the extra effort was on his behalf.

She was still mad at him for ignoring her the whole week. She supposed it was past time he focused on his own life rather than rushing around to take care of hers. But it had still stunned her when he didn't show up on Monday.

They'd talked about Monday, right?

Not really. She'd blown him a kiss, that was all. She'd been the one to mention Monday, and only because she could hardly wait to say the words.

Jax, I love you.

She'd recited them enough times. Surely they'd come out of her mouth this time, and hopefully somewhat coherently. But then Tuesday, Wednesday and Thursday had gone by and she'd heard nothing from him. She couldn't bring herself to call him. She didn't know whether to be relieved or furious when he'd finally phoned her on Thursday evening. She'd responded with a little of both.

Yes, it was the twenty-first century and she had a cell phone. She could just as easily have called him, or shown up at his ranch, for that matter. But something felt different. She couldn't put her finger on it, but she could sense it and it made her feel that the decision to reach out had to come from him.

She was half-afraid he was going to rescind his feelings for her. Maybe that's why she never quite pushed the call button when she started to dial Jax's number.

She checked the clock on the stove. A quarter past six. She still had some chores to do in the barn, and she wanted to bring out some oats for Prada. Being a new mommy, the mare could use the extra nutrition, and Faith figured she might as well spoil Prada while her filly was being examined by the vet.

She looked at her cell phone only a half dozen more times before seven o'clock rolled around—and then passed by. The clock displayed one minute past the hour, then two.

Jax was late, and he was never late. Maybe the vet was one of those guys who was never on time, or maybe there had been some kind of animal emergency.

And then she heard the roaring of dozens of truck engines coming down the road that bordered her house. She frowned, hoping the noise wouldn't bother her herd.

What was going on, anyway?

She was even more surprised when the trucks started pulling into her driveway, all laden with two-by-fours and circular saws and huge cans of paint. Someone had made a big mistake. They had to be looking for a neighbor's house. It looked as if everyone in town was going to this shindig, and she wondered that she hadn't heard about it. She'd been to Cup O' Jo's twice this week. That's usually where she heard all about the latest upcoming social event.

She went out to tell someone they were in the wrong place when Jax strode up, a baby car seat in each arm.

"Sorry we're late. It took me a little longer than usual to dress Violet and Rose."

She glanced down at the babies, who were

each covered with frills and ribbons. Rose in a rose-colored dress and Violet in violet.

"Making it easy for the neighbors?" she teased.

He grinned. "Something like that."

"Well, they look very nice. But speaking of neighbors—do you know where all of these people are headed? They mistakenly pulled into my driveway, and I'm not sure where to direct them."

"Oh, don't worry about that. I've got it covered."

She raised a brow. "Meaning?"

Alice approached with a wide smile. "Come on, Faith, darling. You're the guest of honor." Alice laced her arm through Faith's and led her away from Jax, who just stood there grinning like an idiot.

She looked at Alice, who led her up to one of the rocking chairs on the porch. "I don't know what that means."

"What that means, my dear," said Jo Spencer, pressing Faith into the chair, "is that you get to sit back and watch while we fix up this ol' house of yours."

"I'm sorry?" She couldn't help but stare at the gregarious redhead's T-shirt, which read My Horse Is a Mustang.

"It's our latest community service project.

We've got everything—the tools, the materials and, most important, lunch."

She was about to say she didn't take charity, but Untamed Mustang Refuge actually *was* a charity, so technically that wasn't a feasible argument. A workday on the land or fence-mending might be in order, but—

"My *house*?"

"You'd be surprised at what the townspeople can do in one day. We'll have it looking as good as new," Alice assured her. "Jax even bought some new furniture."

"He did what?"

"Oops," Jo said, covering her giggle with her palm. "I guess we let the cat out of the bag. Was it supposed to be a surprise?"

"This whole thing is a surprise."

"My son did well, then." Alice's voice was full of pride, and Faith supposed it should be, if Jax had organized the entire event.

She was glad she was sitting down because she was beginning to feel a bit overwhelmed. She pressed her palms to her eyes, wondering if someone had a paper bag she could breathe into.

"You don't look so good. Are you feeling okay?" Jax's lyrical voice actually sounded worried.

"I'm feeling overwhelmed, is what I'm feeling. You didn't think it might be a good idea to mention the *entire town* was going to be visiting me today?"

He gave her a once-over and smiled appreciatively. "What are you worried about? You look great today."

She blushed. She *had* dressed up for him. A little. It was nice that he noticed.

"You don't have to worry about a thing. We've got it all under control."

"I can see that," she replied wryly.

He ignored her tone. "The ladies will be setting up lunch pretty soon. I can guarantee you it will be the best country cooking you have ever tasted."

"This is all nice. But why me?"

"Why not you? You put every bit of your effort into your horses. The least we can do is see that you and your home are taken care of, as well."

His gaze warmed and so did her heart. She'd known she belonged in Serendipity from the very first day she was here, the day she'd bid on a big, brooding cowboy with a heart of gold.

"I have to go now since I'm—" He paused. "Kind of in charge of organizing this." Before she could get a word in, he said, "But I'll be back as soon as I can. In the meantime, grab yourself a lemonade and try to enjoy the day."

"Jax?"

He turned back to her.

"What about the vet? Is he even coming, or did you just make that up?"

"Oh, he's coming. Around lunchtime, I think. He loves a good meal."

"But he'll look at the filly, right?"

Jax smiled. "Of course. I'm not going to let that little girl down. I had the privilege of seeing her be born. Have you named her yet?"

"No. I thought maybe we could name her together."

"Great idea. I'll see you at lunch."

She watched Jax walk away, but she lost track of him soon after that. It was hard to make out anyone in particular when everyone was wearing a cowboy hat. At length she took Jax's advice and got a glass of lemonade. She tried to offer to help at the food tables but was promptly turned away.

Everyone seemed to know that this was *her day*—even people she hadn't met before. She wondered exactly what Jax had told them. Whatever it was, it must have been good.

She wandered around, watching folks thatching her roof and painting her barn. It actually looked quite nice after it had been painted in the red and white colors it was supposed to be. Almost like something off a country calendar.

She was surprised when Frank Spencer, Jo's husband, approached her and pulled her aside.

"Now, I know you have a nice big sign out in front of your ranch," he said in a gruff but friendly voice. "But I thought maybe you'd like to have something to hang over your barn, so I—uh—well, here. Take this."

He pointed to a large, tissue-wrapped package lying next to the side of the barn and walked away without another word. Curious, she pulled back the tissue to find a handmade burned-wood carving.

Untamed.

She swallowed hard but the tears still came. This wasn't about fixing up an old house or painting a barn. It was about a community accepting her as their own, and not just her, but the horse rescue she represented.

She was certain there was no better feeling in the world.

She tried to find Frank to thank him for his thoughtful gift, but he had disappeared. A few minutes later, Jo pulled her aside, letting her know lunch was about to begin.

"Folks," she called, loud enough to get the

attention of those closest around her. From there, people continued calling and whistling until everyone was looking at Jo—and at Faith.

She was beginning to understand how Jax must have felt up on that auction block.

"Today we're celebrating with our new neighbor, Faith Dugan. As most of you know, she has put a great deal of time and effort into getting this here mustang refuge up and running. I'm sure I can speak for her when I say she appreciates all that you've done for her today. And if you're feeling so inclined, she could also use a little cash to help with the horses' upkeep and in fixing up her land that was recently burned. She didn't ask for that, by the way. I extemporized." Jo laughed heartily at her own joke, but Faith noticed that Frank had reappeared and was passing his hat. People were reaching into their pockets just as surely as if it was a Sunday morning offering.

"I know everyone is ready to dig in to all this great food," Jo continued, to a big round of applause. "But there's one more item on our agenda."

The crowd parted, and Faith saw Jax at the corral gate. He and the vet were crouched over the little chestnut filly. Jax looked up and grinned, then motioned for her to join him.

She held her breath. How could the new-born foal have anything to do with—*whatever* was going on?

"Vet says she checks out good," Jax told her, loud enough for everyone to hear.

She questioned him with her eyes, but he was giving nothing away. He just kept smiling.

"That's—nice." She wished she'd read this script in advance. She had no idea what she was supposed to say.

"I was thinking we might want to name her. This seems like as good a day as any." He said it in such an offhand way she would have believed he was just making casual conversation, except for the fact that they were surrounded by the entire population of Serendipity and they were all watching avidly.

"I thought maybe Rose and Violet could help us pick out the perfect name."

"O-kay."

"Mama? Jo? Will you please bring the babies out here?"

The two ladies didn't need to be told twice. She'd never seen Jo Murphy walk so fast, and even Alice, with her arthritis, was moving at a clipped pace. The animation in their faces was a dead giveaway to—something.

They put the babies down in front of Faith and stepped away. She looked at Jax, wondering what she was supposed to do. It wasn't as if the babies were going to tell her a name.

Or were they?

She remembered the first time she'd seen the twins, so sweet and vulnerable as they waited for their daddy to come rescue them.

They hadn't had names. She and Jax had searched them for notes. She bent down and brushed her hand through Rose's ruffled dress.

Sure enough, there was a note there, folded in half and fastened with a diaper pin. She laughed as she removed it and waved it for the crowd's benefit. She was about to open it when Jax stopped her.

"Wait. Get Violet's note first. It'll make more sense if you have both of the notes together."

This whole thing was making less than no sense to Faith, but she went along for the ride, feeling as if she was taking part in some larger-than-life baby-shower game, with diaper pins and newborn foals.

She stood with a folded note in each hand. "Can I open them now?"

Jax jammed his hands into the front pockets of his blue jeans. "Yeah. Yes. Open them now."

Faith didn't know what she expected, but she thought the notes would at least be in English. Or maybe they were, but there was only a single letter on each note.

V.

V? V.V.? What was that supposed to stand for?

"You want to call the horse V.V.?" she asked, confused.

Jax burst into laughter. "They aren't letters, Faith. It's a picture."

She looked at the notes again, trying without success to figure out what in the world he was talking about. She glanced up to ask Jax to give her another hint, but he was no longer standing.

He was kneeling, with a diamond ring in his hand.

"Get it?" He grinned.

She glanced around her, totally flustered. Every eye in the place was on her. She didn't know whether she should address the notes in her hand or the name of the filly or—

Oh.

Jax was still on one knee.

The two notes—put them together and they made a diamond.

Jax stood and took her hands in his. As always, the gentle giant.

"I don't care what you call the horse," he said, his voice making every nerve in her body sing. "I just want to hear you tell me you'll be my wife."

He held her left hand and poised the ring, then looked at her expectantly.

"I'll be your wife."

He slid the ring on her finger and kissed her, and the entire town cheered for them.

The next half hour was a blur. Jo and Alice physically placed them at the beginning of the lunch line, and they had to accept the well-wishes of everyone.

"We'll have to do this again in—a month?" he whispered suggestively.

"Three. It takes time to plan a wedding."

"Two."

"Deal. You know, though—I'm not sure this is all on the up-and-up, technically speaking."

"How do you figure?" His brow rose upward, as did the adorable half smile that was pulled by his scar. "What did I miss?"

"I *think* you actually didn't ask me to marry you. Technically speaking. It was more like a demand."

"Yeah, that dictator thing. I'll have to work on that."

She kissed his cheek, right over his scar. "I'll help you. I'm sure Rose and Violet don't want a daddy who bosses them around all day."

"You're probably right." He slid his cheek until his lips met hers. "But you missed something, too. I don't think I've yet heard those three little words."

"Wait a sec."

He shook his head. "No, that's not quite right."

"No. I mean, wait a sec. I want to get my head and heart together before I say this. I've been waiting a long time."

She took his head in her hands and brushed her thumbs against the soft whiskers on his cheeks. "Jackson McKenna, I love you, and there is nothing I want more in the world than to become your wife and the stepmother of your children."

His smile made the wait worthwhile.

"Mother," he corrected. "You are the girls' mother."

"I accept," she whispered, thinking that at that very moment, her life was absolutely perfect.

Except for one thing.

"You know," she said, "we forgot something else in all this excitement."

"What's that? I've got my future bride by my side and my beautiful daughters making the rounds with the neighbors. What else could I possibly want?"

"You did say we were going to name the filly. I think we ought to make that official, too, don't you?"

"Right. The filly. So what do you want to name her, sweetheart?"

She took her time with the answer, simply enjoying the warmth radiating from her future husband's chocolate-brown eyes. Basking in the feeling of loving completely and being loved completely in return. Scars and all.

"Are you going to tell me or do I have to guess?" he prompted between repeated kisses.

"Why, I thought you already knew," she said with a laugh. "Her name is Diamond, of course."

* * * * *

Dear Reader,

Welcome back to Serendipity, Texas. I'm so happy you've joined me for the fourth novel in my Cowboy Country series. I'm thrilled to be able to write the stories I love—rugged cowboys, sweet babies and the resilient women whose commitment makes their lives and families complete. And as always, it's a blessing to revisit Serendipity and all the delightful folks who live there.

Unfortunately, the plight of wild mustangs in this country is a very real tragedy and refuges like Faith's may be the only hope for the future of these fine animals. The Bureau of Land Management has been rounding up a great number of wild horses and burros and placing them in "temporary" holding facilities. But they can't adopt out as many horses as they've contained and the results are devastating, including inhumane roundup practices, poor holding facilities and even mass slaughter.

If we're not careful, the beautiful herds of wild horses that roam the country in freedom will no longer exist, and that will be a real shame and tragedy indeed.

I hope this book has stirred up your interest in mustangs and what can be done on their behalf. For more information I encourage you to visit my sister's charity website, http://www.happyhavenfarm.org, or visit a rescue near you.

I'm always delighted to hear from you, dear readers, and I love to connect socially. You can find my website at http://www.debkastnerbooks.com. Come join me on Facebook at http://www.facebook.com/debkastnerbooks, or you can catch me on Twitter, @debkastner.

Please know that I pray for each and every one of you daily.

Love courageously,

Deb Kastner